REFLECTIONS II
- in words and proverbs

George Manus

1

2.Edition

Author: George Manus
Copyright: George Manus
Design and layout: Ole Praud
Vignettes: Morten Løfberg
Copyright cover: Jan Arnt

Print: BoD - Books on Demand, Norderstedt, Germany
Editor: BoD - Books on Demand, Copenhagen, Denmark (BoD.dk)
e-mail: george.manus@maxmanus.com

Other books written by George Manus:

THOUGHTS, English
TANKER, Norwegian

REFLECTIONS I, English
REFLEKSJONER I, Norwegian

REFLEKSJONER II, Norwegian

REFLECTIONS III, Englisk
REFLEKSJONER III, Norwegian

A WOMAN'S MANY MIGRATIONS, English
EN KVINNES MANGE FLYTTINGER, Norwegian

INNOVATIONS AND CREATIONS, English

70 YEARS IN COMMUNICATION- about the MAX MANUS Companies, English
70 ÅR I KOMMUNIKASJON - om MAX MANUS firmaene, Norwegian

2017

ISBN: 9788771884159

Foreword

These "REFLECTIONS II" are dedicated to my grandsons Oscar and Nicolas.

My earlier reflections I called "REFLECTIONS I", despite they where a mixture of pure reflections and stories.

Perhaps it would have been better to organise them differently, but I have chosen to follow the same pattern in this book. Thus its title "REFLECTIONS II".

They are solely meant to be my own personal reflections and are not to be seen in any way as reliable references.

I believe the stories speak for themselves and as regards these, I will only say that since they mainly go back a very long time, I can't always vouch for their accuracy and correct dating.

Otherwise they are presented as I recall them and probably not without a certain bias.

They where put on paper from 2010 to 2014

Only lately have I got the inspiration to put them together and finished the book, so therefore it has now been published as the 2nd Edition.

To provide the reader with some background stuff of a personal character, I have chosen to begin these "REFLECTIONS II" with my own ego presentation: "No future without a past", which was first given at my Rotary Club in 1987.

As before, I thank Anne Schild for her help with the language, Morten Løfberg for his vignettes, Jan Arnt for the book cover, and my friend Ole Praud for his invaluable consultancy work.

The South of Spain 2017
George Manus
e-mail: george.manus@maxmanus.com

No Future without a Past 6

11-12-13 18

Accusations 21

Advertising 25

Ambitions 29

Communication 32

Compromise 36

Conscience 39

Consequences 42

Curiosity 48

Dependence 51

Experience 55

Feelings 58

Human Development 61

Ignorance 65

Imagination and Creativity 68

In all Honesty 71

Intuition 73

Laughter 77

Looking out for number one 81

Negligence 85

Nicolas' Confirmation Speech 90

Opinions 94

Oscar's Confirmation Speech 98

Prestige 102

San Roque 106

Secret 109

Stories from Landøya 113

The Rolls of Film 114

The Duck Pond 114

The Lawnmower 115

The Executioner's Assistant 117

Bog Hill 118

Grandfather 120

The Linoleum Floor   123
The Gondola Lift   125
The English setter, Pet   128
Reflex   130
The Barn   133
The Garage   135
That's what I've always said   139
The Breithorn   142
The Chin   151
The Conductor   154
The Driving Licence   158
The Grandchild   163
The Hair   165
The Hand   169
The Mouth   171
The Neck   173
The Nose   176
Transitions and Milestones   179
Understanding   182

No Future without a Past

Ego Presentation given at Furuset Rotary Club in 1987

Dear Rotarians and guests.

An indisputable prerequisite for growing up is having been born. The date was 14.5.1939, very early in the morning. As in all mothers' lives, it was surely a big event. The following probably applies here as well as in other situations:

"Most women give birth to children, but only I give birth to mine".

The offspring was very thin according to what I've been told, but we can't all be the same.

The place of confinement was the local hospital at Caterham, a suburb of London.

To be brief, my maternal grandfather, the County Governor in Bergen and Hordaland, felt that his daughter, after finishing her A-levels at Bergen Katedralskole, ought to learn languages. London was chosen and the year was, as far as I know, 1933.

What actually happened was that she met the man who was later to become her husband. He was English and one of three brothers. He ran a family business which was founded in 1885 and which was responsible for the unloading of wood from all Scandinavian countries, a so-called Stevedore firm.

The wedding took place in 1936. They built a house in Caterham and though a lot of it was exciting, I don't think my mother really settled down to being a stay-at-home housewife in England. She drove her husband to the local train station every morning and picked him up in the afternoon, after having spent most of the day playing bridge with other like-minded women. That was apparently how one had to live at the time, and the English are conservative.

I was, as mentioned, born in 1939. The heavy clouds over Europe, which we have all heard of, seemed to be extra heavy at the time, because mother shortly after moved back to Bergen with me.

Allegedly the thin offspring was also quite ill at the time. The doctors weren't sure what illness I had, but that I was going to die there was apparently no doubt at all.

The medicine which finally cured the evil was said to have been tried for the first time in Norway on yours truly. Drama from the word go, and as if that wasn't enough, while staying at Ulvik in Hardanger, the family hotel was set on fire by the Germans. The old wooden hotel burnt down to the ground and the baby carriage with me in it was apparently rescued at the last minute.

My father reported for duty at the Foreign Office after his elder brother was killed in Ethiopia. The import of wood in England had stopped because of the war and the firm was closed. It's probably a bit strange that he despite being an officer in one of England's oldest regiments, The Honourable Artillery Company, considering the lack of officers in those days, was transferred to Haugesund as Consul. He had, however, fairly good knowledge of Scandinavia and spoke a bit of Norwegian. He was - among other duties - to report on the movements of the German fleet.

The Germans came and he retreated towards the north and ended up in Åndalsnes. The house he was staying in there got hit by German bombers.

It's not easy to make the story short, but I'll try. He was rescued from the ruins as a non-survivor, but someone must have seen that he was still alive.

He was later transferred to the hospital in Ålesund, heavily wounded by metal splinters in his head.

Via Vollan prison in Trondheim he was then by the Germans sent to Møllergata 19 in Oslo.

During one of his stays at Ullevål Hospital in Oslo my mother visited him and that was actually the first time she heard the name, Max Manus. This strange person had fled from his guards at the same hospital the night before, after first having struck down a nurse. My mother and Max were to meet later on in life and there is no doubt that my life has also been affected by that meeting.

My father was, due to his diplomatic status, eventually sent to Sweden and was there operated several times by the well-known brain surgeon, Olivenkrona.

The metal splinters were removed after which he spent a long time recovering at Saltsjøbaden outside Stockholm.

My life as a hostage began after Fehmer, himself the the top German Gestapo officer in Oslo, gave the order that if my mother wanted to go to

Stockholm, she would have to leave me in Norway.

My dear auntie Kari, mother's sister, had due to the war moved from Bergen to Ulvik in Hardanger. She became my mother number two and a person I greatly appreciated. Unfortunately she died a few years ago. My mother's brother, Sjur, became part of the resistance movement from the very beginning, whereas my maternal grandfather stayed in his post as County Governor throughout the war. It seemed to be the way things went in those days.

It's been reported that the hostage in Ulvik wasn't very old before he was given an extra ration at the co-op, because of the excuse he used: "You must take pity on me because I haven't got a mother or a father".

In Stockholm my mother worked at the British Legation, where she under the nickname "Auntie", among other things, wrote and conveyed reports from the resistance people who managed to get to Sweden on their way to England. She was later given King Haakon's Medal of Freedom for her work, of which she is very proud.

As I have been told by my mother, a very strange man by the name of Max Manus appeared at the office one day, after one of his resistance operations in his homeland. It must have been this meeting which was to be the start of a new future. It is said that time solves most problems and there is certainly a lot of truth in that. I don't know why, because nobody has been able to tell me why, but the hostage was eventually set free at a later date, with the natural consequence that he ended up at his mother's, again as when he was born, abroad. Some insignificant confusions of time may have sneaked in here, but no matter how it was; the earlier hostage had become a big boy all at once.

After my stay in Stockholm, back to Ulvik in Hardanger I went, where my first school year finished the spring I turned seven.

The reason for my early start was probably that the extra work for my auntie Kari was reduced by letting me start school rather than having me at home. Her daughter and son were already at school.

The teacher was another aunt, though not by blood, and she accepted responsibility for me. She died many years ago, but I still remember her as a somewhat special person.

I can also remember that I went to Sunday school the same year and got a good many stars in my book.

Somewhere in time, just after the liberation in 1945, I recall one of the biggest disappointments imaginable, the taste of my first banana. There was no end to my tears, the banana had been so much talked about and so overrated, and then for me there was no taste.

Back to Sweden once more and what do I remember from those days that may have affected me? At least one episode from the tail end of this stay in Sweden, I can recall; too terrible. Without having any other purpose than lighting a fire, I managed to light one in a wood stove standing in a barracks consisting of at least two storeys. I lit the fire on purpose, of course, but what I didn't know was that the stove had no chimney. The result of it being that the entire house burnt down to the ground.

Furthermore, I lost my watch one day at the daycare centre. It had been given to me by my father and I never forgot its loss.

The summer of 1945, was perhaps the start of that part of my life which was seriously concerned with my development and awareness of environmental influence.

The middle of the day, lovely sunshine, I recall. The place being a summer camp way out in the Swedish country-side. A car arrives with my mother and an unknown man inside. My belongings were packed and off we went. I became carsick at the time and have been frequently so ever since.

There was apparently a lot of excitement at the Norwegian border; I had some odd thoughts, but was to young to understand. Had my father, who was a convalescent but who still had his position as Vice-Consul in Stockholm, heard tell about a kidnap attempt?

Had he been able to arrange for us to be stopped at the border? No, not at all, everything went well and the kidnap victim didn't understand a thing.

It later came to me, that my mother's female instincts must have been quite natural, I had to be part of the deal.

After the mentioned stay at auntie Kari's in Ulvik, I ended up at Landøya in Asker, a place Max had bought just after the liberation.

There I lived until I got married. Max turned into uncle Max and a more orderly life took shape, though perhaps not always welcome from my point of view.

At seven I started my second school year at Holmen school.

The problem - no, even in those days problems became challenges - was that I spoke a mixture of Ulvik dialect and Swedish.

This was the most important reason for my day mainly consisting of my strength being tested. We humans just seem to be made that way.

The school almost became a story in itself. Bible history, geography and normal history, I understood in part, but in other subjects I was hopelessly bad.

I never actually had to repeat a year, but seldom was anyone closer to doing so than me. It was said that the most positive part of what I did at school was that I spoke loudly and clearly in class, but my teacher pointed out that I suffered from something which today would probably be called a mild form for dyslexia. I read, as I've said, loudly and clearly but only partly from the book. At least half of what I read aloud was pure invention, nicely fitting into the whole, a fact only discovered by those who paid attention to the every written word.

Uncle Max, who was trying to make a man out of the rabble arouser, cheered for the other side when unavoidable fights got started. This was a therapy which I am sure was well-meant but didn't always feel positive.

Anyway, especially problematic I can't remember my life as being especially problematic and much of my treatment was probably my own fault. At least one extra page of the manuscript would be needed to cover a summary of things which deserved punishment.

The property at Landøya was big and thinking back, there is no doubt that Max took part in a lot of fun and games and that he let our gang of boys have a lot of freedom at play.

My father, whom I had last seen just before leaving Sweden, I next met when I at eleven took the train to Stockholm on my own. He was still convalescent, had epilepsy from his injuries, but even so had just got married again to a Swedish woman. What do I actually remember from this meeting? Of course, the visit to Grøna Lund, and my father, but mainly the return train journey which ended up being very special.

There was a major derailment of great dimension at Pålsboda in Sweden, where thirty or forty people ended up in hospital and where at least one person was killed if I remember correctly. I was woken by the conductor who couldn't open the door to my compartment. My car was the fourth having derailed, while the engine and the cars in front had been thrown into complete chaos.

Three years later I again met my father. This time on Jersey in the Channel Islands, where he had settled with his wife and their first little daughter. This was my first big trip abroad on my own. Oslo, Bergen, Newcastle, London and then by plane from Southampton to Jersey.

Twenty years would pass before I saw him again.

Back to 1947, my brother Max was born followed two years later by my sister Mette. We have always been, and still are, good friends.

A guide for growing up: Freedom with responsibility, a system which seldom failed. I suffered the occasional slip, of course, but never intentionally.

I feel that I have a fair judgement of what is right and what is wrong, honest and dishonest.

Max was involved in the organizing of the Home Guard from the very beginning after the war and thus it was quite natural for him to include me. I started as a sporadic staff driver at Home Guard manoeuvres at fourteen or fifteen, so there was never a dull moment.

In all manner of Home Guard manoeuvres, "playing at war" was my only form of military service, but it was exciting.

Sport also formed part of my life and here it went far better than at school.

I took part in cross country skiing, ski-jumping, shooting, ice-hockey and a bit of sailing, but I lacked the will to win. The nerves failed, the hero seldom reached the top, but it was said that he had innate abilities for most things.

With girls, however, it was far easier, for some reason it wasn't so difficult to concentrate in this area.

All told, I did my O-levels and went to business school, and there was never any question of a higher education in my case. The practical suited me far better. Technical problems, carpentry and mechanics were more up my street; there my abilities were in order.

My summer job for several years was thus to work in the Max Manus Office Machine Company's workshop. The firm was in those days general agent in Norway for Olivetti office machines among others. It thus seemed natural to send me to their school in Italy. As they were by far Europe's largest factory of its kind at the time, they had their own school for the technical side as well as sales and administration.

In 1956 I went to the town of Ivrea in Northern Italy and this became my home for just over a year. I followed technical training on all types of typewriters and calculators. The classes I was placed in consisted of nothing but Italians who had nothing much in the way of any common language skills.

So I learnt to babble away in Italian after only a few months. The stay there and the subsequent half a year or so at business school in Florence, followed by short stays of practical training at the various Olivetti branches throughout Italy, strike me as the most important period of my personal development.

On my eighteenth birthday which I celebrated down there, I sold my Vespa scooter and bought a car. The deal gave me a profit of about a hundred kroner which more or less covered the cost of my driving licence on my eighteenth birthday. I had, after all, been able to drive earlier.

Back home, I started to train the firm's many technicians, and later I went deeper into the running of the firm, but that's another story.

As with many others in my group of friends, I ended up getting married early. It seemed to be in the nature of things, an early start in a full-time job meant it was time to start a family. At barely twenty-one,

I was, of course, master of the universe, knew everything, and didn't let anything stop me. I had, by the way, been together with my future wife for nearly three years. She was from Oslo and we started our twenty-year marriage in an apartment at Ljabru. This was a bit too far from our friends and we soon, after about a year's stay in Halvdan Svartes gate, moved to a big, old flat at Skillebekk. Here our eldest daughter, Nicoline, named after her paternal grandmother, was born in nineteen sixty-three, followed by Anne-Marie, named after her aunt, in 1965.

Our circle of friends were close-knit, everyone were busy working, but certainly also knew how to enjoy themselves together. There were frequent parties which made the rounds, but everything was based on shared expenses. That way it became possible.

My wife worked for the first few years but later she went to school and took courses in weaving and pictorial art. Our income improved and we travelled frequently in our spare time. We took the children along whenever it was possible.

Throughout the years we frequently visited the family cabin at Filefjell and a year without grouse hunting seemed unthinkable.

In 1970 we moved into our newly built house in Gråkammen at Vettakollen and life took on a familiar pattern. Even though the catchment area was large, we managed to be part of most things; but there is no doubt that something essential was lacking in our relationship. Isn't it said that one grows apart? Our relationship did after a while develop a list and finally sank in 1979.

My father, whom I'd last seen and heard from when I visited him at the age of fourteen, I met again after having found him once more sometime in seventy-five.

It probably sounds strange that we hadn't had any contact during all these years, blood is after all thicker than water, but I had to turn thirty-five before I was mature enough to re-establish contact. He was then living in Spain.

It was a wonderful visit and what did I encounter? As many as three half-sisters. A couple of twins, who had just finished an engagement as dancers in the Bluebell troupe at the Lido in Paris and their somewhat elder sister.

All three were more than one metre eighty tall and the founder of the Bluebells had apparently kept an eye on the twins, as at least one of them had danced ballet during her adolescence in Jersey. Today two of them are married and have children. They live in London and Paris respectively, while the third lives in Hamburg.

My father, who is now seventy-five, I meet more or less annually, which is a pleasure for both of us. He is a resident of Jersey but spends most of the year in Spain.

From being someone who didn't have either mother or a father, to becoming someone who has two mothers, two fathers and five siblings, has probably also had a great influence on me.

As a person, I'm not as extroverted as I may seem and I've always been reluctant to stand out. The personal image of the firm, I have probably at times taken too seriously, but I also feel that I'm quite good at delegating.

I have been the manager of most of the undertaking for about twenty years; and as manager of our activities in Denmark for the last ten years,

During this time I've had ample opportunity to study human behaviour in these two countries, and thus gained great respect for integrity. I'm very much aware of the need to provide proper conditions permitting individual expression.

On the sport side, I have been on the board of Norway's Rifle Association's Clay Pigeon Division and have since nineteen seventy-two been foreman in the Skeet Club, a club which does clay pigeon shooting.

For a short time I've been on the board of Oustøen Country Club, which concerns itself with golf. Since the beginning of the seventies I have, when it comes to sport, concentrated on clay pigeon shooting, bird hunting and golf.

I'm living in a world where I believe in the power of example and even if it's difficult at times in basic goodness of mankind.

I'm still a member of a few boards but have really enough with my own business.

An example which I would still like to mention though is that I, for the last couple of years, have had the pleasure of being a member of the board and joint owner of a newly founded firm in Denmark, which is based on an old idea of mine, which I nurtured for several years. It was something so simple yet as complex as air. In this case an inflatable neck pillow which we called Sleepover.

It is apparently a product people want and which this year represents an export worth more than thirteen million Danish kroner.

I only mention this because through my own involvement I have gained an insight into a totally different kind of business. The people involved, not least in distribution, are very different from those I normally associate with, and the fact that sales take place on all continents fascinates me.

I believe I can be characterized as a very monogamous man. Some will say that it was planned, but in that case it must have been from a higher level, which I myself don't discount.

It so happened that only a few weeks after the dissolution of my marriage, my secondary school had an anniversary celebration. I met again an old flame of mine who had broken up with me back then and who was now herself a widow. Her time had come.

We have been together for the last six years, but are not married. Her two children are grown up. The son is starting his military service at Christmas, while the daughter, at twenty-three, is studying at Blindern University.

My ex-wife has moved to Spain, so it seemed natural for my daughters to stay with me after the divorce.

The younger one, Anne-Marie, went to college in Switzerland and completed three years there, whereas Nicoline after an intermediary year at college in England, completed the Trade Gymnasium in Oslo. The two of them spent a year together at school in Paris in nineteen eighty-three and four, and then had a year at home, where the younger one took the secretarial course at the Trade Gymnasium and the elder sister did the first of two years at Sverre Wolf's school of decoration. She completed the course there this year, while Anne-Marie started at the University of St. Louis in Madrid, where the idea is to study for two years and then move on to the U.S. for the final two years. The relationships between all of us in our new family situation function brilliantly.

As for me, I have throughout all these years kept my British citizenship, not that it gives me any personal benefits, but there has always been something in me which hasn't felt wholly Norwegian.

The world undeniably consist of far more than Norway and even though it at times has caused a bit of personal turbulence, I have a strong belief that if we want to live in a world at peace, it can only happen by opening the doors and going out there getting to know other people and cultures.

Finally I'd like to say that I feel happyl at Rotary, and even though I know that I can't dedicate enough time to my work here, I feel that the ideals of the organization go hand in hand with my own views on life's values.

Thank you for your attention.

In 1994, after seven years as a member of Furuset Rotary Club and with new members to be considered, there was a request to repeat the ego presentation.

What you have read was repeated, but after thanking the audience for their attention, it lay in the nature of things that something had to be added.

After all, seven more years of my life had gone by. So I added the following:

Had it only been that simple.

Many years have gone by since I wrote this and life continues relentlessly.

My daughter, Nicoline, died of cancer almost four years ago, at the tender age of twenty-seven.

Only those who have experienced this sort of loss, are able to understand what it means.

My biological father, who really shouldn't have survived 1940, came to a natural end at the age of 83 in February this year.

The firm has seen a lot of hardship over the last few years, with major cutbacks and restructuring and I won't hide the fact that it's been a great challenge to keep everything going at times.

But life must go on.

Anne-Marie has long since finished her financial education at the university in Madrid. She has joined our firm and it seems that we have overcome our biggest challenges both personally and commercially.

She's living with Jens and seems to be happy, while my common-law wife and I keep finding security in our relationship.

My half-sisters' offspring now come to a total of eight world citizens, from two to eighteen years of age, and together they speak at least five languages fluently and live in four different countries.

The expression which says that adversity makes strong, has for me become a reality and in many ways I feel richer as a person after the events of the last few years.

Thank you for your attention.

New addition 2017 *years have gone by since my ego presentation was held for the first time in 1987.*

20 years have passed since the second and last time in 1994.

These last 20 years form the third phase of my life since my relationship to my then common-law wife came to an end.

The change of scene led to a new relationship which resulted in marriage in 1998.

Anne-Marie, also known as Pøne by those close to her, has long since married her Jens. They took over the running of the firm several years ago and this now operates in Norway, Denmark and Sweden.

My grandsons Oscar and Nicolas are 21 and 19 respectively, and granddad is living the life of an active pensioner with his Swiss wife, Marianne, in the South of Spain.

My job is to create, to find the way. Others will have to level and pave.
GM

The correctness of history deteriorates proportional to the time it takes from it originated to the time it is written down.
GM

Although it is said that the shortest way to the goal is the quickest, it isn't always the best.
GM

11-12-13

December 2013

A small notice in The Times on the 9th of December 2013 says that the special combination 11.12.13, which in this case stands for the date, the 11th of December 2013, is very unusual and that a similar sequence won't happen again until the 1st of February 2103.

Perhaps another small notice will appear at that time, informing people of the event, in other words about 90 years from now; we'll have to wait and see.

I believe most of us have a number or perhaps several, that we consider lucky or perhaps sinister or that we connect to something special.

I'm sitting here by chance on a Friday evening, by chance because I didn't have any plans of putting anything to paper. However, this is how it happens when I get an idea, or more clearly, a title for a "reflection"; I register it, if it's convenient at the time, in a list of suchlike, usually with a headline and a few pointers which will later serve as clues to what I was thinking.

Thus the first paragraph, which was created in the morning of the 10th of December 2013, after I had read the notice in The Times the previous evening.

There's nothing special about this Friday evening other than that I have felt somewhat tired all day. For some reason I didn't get enough sleep the night before. Perhaps because I was unconsciously disturbed by the fact that an acquaintance of ours, who lives only a few hundred meters away, had had a break-in the previous night.

Regardless, my wife suggested early this morning that we perhaps eat lunch out somewhere, after her hour of "Pilates", which she has become quite thrilled about. If you don't know it, I didn't know what "Pilates" was either before I saw a brochure in the reception of our physiotherapist, my wife describes it as "a physical fitness system which very gently does all the joints and muscles in your body some good".

This has nothing to do with numbers, but we had on this occasion chosen a simple restaurant down by the sea where they make a super cheese fondue, and as we sat talking about dates in connection with our impending trip to Portugal at Christmas, we discovered that it was Friday the 13th. A day one usually connects with the opposite of a lucky one.

For those who think this day means the same everywhere, I can tell them that they're wrong. Here in Spain the unlucky day is Tuesday the 13th, just so everyone knows.

Looking at the world as a whole, there are surely a number of different days and dates one has to watch out for or, for that matter, look forward to, according to whether they are said to bring misfortune or good luck.

Can one then prevent possible misfortune on unlucky days or step up one's purchase of lottery tickets, if the day is lucky? I don't think so, if an accident is about to happen, it will and if one wins the lottery, one does, providing, of course, that one has bought a ticket. In that case, it's like fishing, the bated hook must be in the water if one wants to catch fish. If one is conscious of it being Friday the 13th, however, the day supposedly unlucky for some of us, and thus takes a bit of extra care, it might help lower the accident statistics.

The other day I got into a conversation with Paco, a former policeman, who in his old age adds to his pension by selling used golf balls. It is forbidden for outsiders to collect golf balls on our golf course, a rule which, for reasons unknown, applies to everyone except Paco. Why he's in a privileged position, I can't say, but he's a very pleasant person whom we see every day in the car park in his little Peugeot, from which he sells the balls, packed in plastic bags.

Since Spain has an enormous spread of lottery and one of the big draws happened to be on that day, we started talking about it.

It probably sounds incredible, statistically speaking, but Paco told me that he had won the lottery three times. The first time was many years ago, when the peseta was still in use, 100,000, then four years ago 40,000 Euros and last year 20,000.

The truth of this was confirmed later in the pro shop, where the person in charge told me that she already had an agreement with him to buy tickets for the next big draw, "El Gordo".

I see no reason to keep my lucky numbers secret. Everyone may use them in any given situation should they wish to.

They are 14 and 17. Ever since I found out about lucky numbers, I chose these two, but in reserve I also had 7 and 21. Eventually it became too difficult to keep track of them all, so now I stick with just the two.

Have they then been lucky numbers? I haven't always kept track, but have to admit that even though I don't buy tickets or gamble, I still hang on to 14 and 17.

My wife hasn't got any lucky numbers, she says, because she early on in life ascertained that she wasn't a lottery winner.

If the Americans hold Friday the 13th unlucky, as we do, I don't know, but if they do, it will probably be remembered by the investors of that which was called Euro Vegas, an enormous gambling complex with was supposed to be built outside Madrid.

I just watched the Spanish news a moment ago and the government hasn't agreed to their requirements and thus refused to give them a green light for the establishment. One of their requirements was dispensation to smoke in the gambling halls. We'll have to see who gives in and if further negotiations lead to Spain getting a gambling Mecca.

"All good things come in threes" it is said when one thinks positively, whereas the expression "no two without three" is often used about accidents.

The expression "7.9.13" is perhaps not frequently used but is said to be a magic spell against accidents. The expression is a fairly new one according to the experts. 7 has always been a lucky number from what I understand, whereas 9 is loaded with mystery. 13 is considered both a lucky and an unlucky number. The latter is also based on the fact that Judas was the thirteenth at the table with Jesus and the other 11 disciples.

Apropos to my introduction, which describes 11, 12 and 13, I also see another little notice in The Times, but this time in the 13th of December edition, that someone has taken the opportunity to produce a headline: "Marriage? It's a date". A couple who met on the 01.02.03 has taken advantage of this "one time opportunity" to get married on the 11.12.13.

If you don`t cure the basic faults in golf,
you will never become a reasonably good player
GM

Accusations

March 2014

Especially in early childhood and adolescence fairness is an important element in everyone's life. That's because it is in this phase of one's life that one becomes acquainted with fairness for the first time, often in connection with accusations of various kinds, both true and false ones.

As soon as one's upbringing starts to focus on what's right and what's wrong, and that's one of the first things one is confronted with, one becomes acquainted with accusations.

Accusations are a completely natural occurrence in our upbringing.

If one is lucky enough at an early stage in one's development to have a clear concept of what is right and what is wrong, one is indeed lucky, but it can hurt a lot the first time one suffers a false or wrong accusation.

If one is accused of something one has done and knows deep down that one has done it and that it was wrong, other factors are automatic brought in. One has to consider whether one wants to admit to it or not. If one believes that the consequences will be major by making an admission, it's only human, as one can frequently see, to deny the accusations.

Not that I in any way want to defend an improper denial of accusation which are probably "true", but in this context I can't avoid mentioning how widespread this is in Spanish politics.

Hardly a day goes by without the news being filled with so-called political corruption charges. The charges seem, as far as I can judge, to be more or less equally distributed among the various political fractions and what they have in common is that they are all denied at first until they have been proven correct or, which in my opinion happens all to frequently, they remain claims without consequences because not enough proof is ever produced.

The same probably happens in many other countries, but one normally pays more attention to what is happening in the country where one lives.

Lies are probably one of the first things one learns about in life, as one early on has to test how far one can toe the line and what consequences it has when one oversteps it.

Perhaps a separate reflection about the lie would be a good idea, but that'll have to wait until a more suitable occasion.

The false accusation or the incorrect one is the one which really hurts. It can, of course, be based on a lack of information, which might easily have been obtained and thus it helps create even greater misunderstanding.

Case dismissed without further consequences, but if the incorrect accusation is so one-sided and steadfast that it can't be disproved, then things might become dangerous.

I myself was far from an exemplary pupil. Homework was almost non-existent and if I could make mischief, for which I had a great ability, I did. Naturally enough, seen from the point of view of the teachers, it thus became very easy to blame me, even for things I hadn't done. I can't recall any serious charges, but even the few times it happened, it was extremely painful.

The sense of fairness is for most of us a strong one.

Within politics a large portion of the time available to most parties is spent making accusations against one another in the media.

I have noticed this especially here in Spain. Without having made any detailed records, I believe that in all political newscasts on TV , I hears more or less exclusively slanderous accusations against other parties. Highlighting one's own politics in understandable terms is rare.

Anyway, there are bound to be in depth studies made of this phenomenon and the conclusion will surely be that this is the correct procedure in order to achieve success, or else one wouldn't be stupid enough to continue in these enlightened times, would one?

Are we humans really that stupid? In this case the answer has to be a definite "yes".

A lot of people are capable of deliberately accusing someone of something one knows they know they haven't done. In my opinion, there has to be a clear profit motive behind it, or a deep-seated motive of revenge. Or could it be that those who do such things are totally without scruples?

If not, how can it be possible to commit such an injustice?

So-called "justice murder", which are what miscarriages of justice are called in Norwegian, are probably at the top of the list when it comes to incorrect accusations. (According to Wikipedia the expression miscarriage of justice is used when a person has been convicted in a court of law of a crime he or she hasn't committed.)

Originally the Norwegian expression was used when someone was wrongly convicted and sentenced to death, but as this method of punishment became less common or was finally abolished, the expression has been given an extended meaning. The strong word "murder" illustrates the criminal act which contributes to or causes an innocent person to be sentenced and detained.

Fortunately miscarriages of justice don't happen too often, but imagine what a meaningless and desperate situation a person must be in when it does happen. Without wishing to discriminate against the French in general, I must include the details of a recant personal experience.

My wife's newly acquired white-painted Hyundai i30 was parked in its normal place, in front of our apartment, while we were away for a few weeks and had used my car to travel to the airport.

Back home again and almost immediately after we have brought our suitcases inside, the doorbell rings. The caretaker, who also keeps an eye on our apartment when we're away, informs us that he, just a couple of days after we had left, had seen our neighbour, a Frenchman, back his blue-painted car, also a Hyundai but a larger model, out of the car park. By accident or poor judgement, he watched him scrape along the side of my wife's car and leave some heavy blue marks on the white paint. We had already noticed, when we parked after arriving home from the airport, that his car, which before we left had had various small dents on the right side, had been newly painted and was without a scratch.

We knew he had earlier backed into one of the outside lights in the driveway and broken it, but how any new dents had been acquired was, of course, none of our business.

The following day my wife gets in touch with the Frenchman and in her mother tongue which is French, she appraises him of the damage to her car.

To her consternation he denies that he has anything to do with it and points out that his car has been newly painted and is without a scratch. I've seldom seen such nerve, but then he happens to be a very unpleasant person.

Our French neighbour rents the house he's living in and I doubt that he'll ever read this, but should he happen to do so, I hope he'll understand why now we completely ignore him.

We could, of course, have taken him to court, and experienced a lot of frustration as a result, but life is too short for such things at our age.

This is one of those cases where one puts up one's hands and says to oneself:

"Where there is nothing, even the Emperor's power ceases". Here I don't have any material things in mind for the poor man.

People of his kind probably think of themselves as winners; after all, he was spared the expense.

Understanding

Those who think I don't know it-
have evidently not understood-
that things have been let happen-
which I saw should have been halted-
and for the very simple reason-that development takes place
through sacrifice and vision-
not by putting a calculated stop to the mission.

It has cost to sow - the profits have been low-
but it's worth the understanding I have gathered up to now.
GM

Advertising

March 2014

Advertising is only one of the terms used in connection with what we call marketing.

Wikipedia describes advertising as a form of communication the purpose of which is to inform potential customers about products and services, how they can be used and where one can obtain them.

It was practically unknown at home in Norway when I started my professional life at the end of the fifties.

On second thoughts it's definitely not completely correct that advertising was as good as unknown in those days, but the activity connected with it was quite modest compared with the way it is today.

One did, of course, present the names of the firms and the trademarks existing in those days in a way that made the ordinary people, the customers, aware of their existence, but this was done to a much more modest degree, usually outside buildings and in places such as on vehicles, special hoardings and appropriate buildings.

Television had barely reached the country; NRK, then only in black and white, was the only broadcasting channel and not available for advertising purposes.

More channels eventually appeared and later also in colour, so TV advertising consumed a large portion of the advertising budget, at least in the larger firms.

The radio was also a medium which at the time was used to a large extent in advertising.

Advertising hoardings along the roads were, I believe, already forbidden, but I'm not sure.

I also don't remember when neon advertising made its entry, but it always gave me a thrill seeing the Durex ad at the top of Bogstadveien. It has long since given way to the presentation of new products.

Regardless, this subject is, as everyone can understand, infinitely extensive and far from something which I have the necessary requirements to address (as has also been the case with so many other reflections.) Nevertheless, it's important to have an opinion.

Of course, and here I think most of us agree, almost all commercial business needs to be promoted in order to get the economic wheel to turn faster.

Apart from the necessary food products and certain household items that most of us in this so-called developed world are dependent on, plus a few personal articles such as toothbrushes, toothpaste, shaving things, tampons, etc., there are thousands of other articles which never would be bought if the price didn't allow for good margins and so allow advertising and promotion.

Even with basic articles, on which one is more or less dependent, there is considerable competition between the various suppliers, in order to secure the largest possible share of the market.

Several years ago I wrote a reflection about "Price". It concerned itself with the fact that one often highlights the price of a product as being the best selling point when it comes to buying it. Put a different way, one sometimes gets the impression that the need for the product itself is not under discussion, and that the entire dialogue between the seller and the potential buyer is concerned only with the price, discounts and terms of payment.

Some manufacturers, and I believe this is the case within most industries, have had and still have the ability to produce items which distance themselves from others in the opposite direction, that is to say with prices that are sky high.

Vanity, prestige and association with quality are probably the prime reason for such products obtaining a wider market than just the rich alone. For example there are brand name clothes and capital products such as cars, boats and expensive watches.

In a country like Norway, with a generally high standard of living and a relatively large number of well-to-do households, inevitably there is a real market for highly priced quality products.

Do we become blinded by, or should I say, mesmerized by many marketing campaigns? I feel that it is so, as otherwise I can't understand what's happening.

If one takes as one example out of many, the Rolex watch concept, and try to imagine the enormous amount of money they spend on marketing in form of sponsoring agreements, advertising campaigns and TV commercials, one has to ask oneself where the money comes from. The products are, of course, in the upper price bracket but, even so, they are no more than fifty or a hundred times the price of ordinary watches. It would be interesting to know the cost of producing these watches compared with others in a more reasonable bracket.

There is an advantage that one can dive down several hundred meters with some of these watches *on* without destroying them and they are, of course, very elegant, no doubt about that.

I think this narrows down to the fact that it is prestige which makes it possible to achieve a market position like the one they have and prestige isn't just something one is handed on a plate. It takes time to build, costs a lot and requires a certain attitudes.

I have from so-called reliable sources heard that they, Rolex that is, don't earn their money from their watches, but it is their involvement in the property market which makes it successful, It would certainly be impressive if this were true.

Not that it means anything, but I myself am an Omega man, thanks to a gift given to me on my sixtieth birthday. It has been impeccably reliable for fifteen years, whereas the metal strap had to be changed after about ten years. The latter was probably because I always wear it when I play golf.

Thinking of the big names in golfing equipment, who sponsor the top players with hundreds of millions and the fact that a set of golf clubs for instance costs less than a good dinner for four in a Norwegian restaurant, I can't avoid asking myself how this is possible, how they manage to balance their books.

There are I believe something like seventeen thousand golf courses and more than thirty million players in the USA, but it remains a puzzle.

What does it actually cost to produce such a golf set? Copies and pirate versions one can buy for a fraction of the proper price, but they don't have the right name nor do they sponsor any of the big names within the sport.

Top golfers are not made by the products they espouse.

For the average golfer there are only marginal differences in the effect the equipment has on the results, but it's always good to have something to believe in, or for that matter to put the blame on.

During my time in the office machine industry, the goal of our firm was to spend 5 % of the turnover on marketing initiatives. As turnover goes up and down in all industries it was not always possible to maintain the same percentage, but our objective was clear.

Exhibitions took a large slice of the budget, while newspaper advertising and, later in the seventies, TV *advertising* became an important part of our marketing initiatives.

Repeatedly we had our logo, the two red elephants, encircling various English football venues, covering those football pool matches which were always popular at that time in Norway. We also used the radio to advertise our intercom systems.

Perhaps it's now a sign of maturity, we are after all in our "vintage years", that we constantly have to admit to ignorance over what is being advertised when probably quite ingenious TV clips offer some product or other for sale. Those who have sold their ingenious ideas to their taskmasters have probably left our generation out of the equation, as uninteresting customers.

Well, I'll be seventy-five in a couple of months and I bought my latest golf set less than a year ago. This happened without the influence of the media, but based on the opinion of a friend and able golfer. He is, however, ten years younger than me and has probably not lived through the same TV golf clips, because those - even those - we can understand.

There are movements so simple and efficient that they must be taken seriously.
GM

Ambitions

April 2013

Not everyone possesses a competitive spirit. This, among other things, is what ambition stands for, "the desire to compete, aspiration". It all has to do with oneself. As with prestige, it is something personal. But it does not necessarily have the same negative connotations as prestige in my opinion.

"The desire to compete, aspiration", I see here not necessarily as being in competition with others.

I choose, at least for the time being, to look at wanting to compete, as something one wants to do for oneself, compete with oneself and whatever ambitions one might have in a given situation.

Here the driving force comes into it again. Where there's no driving force, it's difficult to find progress.

Of course lots of people are happy without having ambitions. Why do so many people see being without ambition as something negative? Imagine what the world would be like if everyone had limitless ambition?

I think we all agree that not everyone can be academically inclined. What about the countless number of service jobs needed to get the world to function? It shouldn't, in any way, mean that one is worth less or lacks ambition just because one isn't academically inclined.

Society ought to function in such a way, that those who have personal ambitions should basically be able to achieve them.

Take, for instance, young people with political ambitions.

These ambitions are probably influenced by their homes or environments. If one has abilities or ambitions to do with politics, I don't think there's any reason to suppose lack of support.

Regardless of political party, one is welcomed with open arms.

A good example of this, is the tragic event at Utøya in Norway on July 22, 2011.

Already at the end of the fifties, I can recall that every time we drove past the Tyrifjord on our way to the family cabin at Filefjell, mentioned was made of the island being the location of the Norwegian socialist hatchery. Everyone knew that this was the starting point for all those who wanted to become someone within the labour party. All Norwegian socialist top leaders have, as long as I've been aware of things, risen through the ranks by making regular visits to this island. I had no special political ambitions at that time, nor have I really had any later on, but we were aware of what was going on.

I've also never hidden the fact that my political stance is somewhat more to the right.

All the young people gathered there on that fatal summer's day, had their own political ambitions and deserve our full respect for that.

Mr. Breivik's ambitions, on the other hand, were of the worst kind. Madness is probably a more correct description than just twisted political ambitions.

Sporting ambitions; as long as they are only on one's own behalf, it is both necessary and correct to have. If one's ambition is to reach the topthen so many self-denials and sacrifices are necessary, that if one isn't motivated and has steel-clad ambitions, one simply doesn't reach one's goal.

Worse are parents' ambitions for their children.

I begin with some personal experiences from my early days in business.

Already before I turned twenty, at the end of the fifties, I was responsible for the training of approximately 40 technicians.

Even then, I noticed that many of those who already had families, fought hard to give their children an education they felt they themselves had not been able to get due to the war.

It was a matter of course, that if it hadn't been for the war, they would all have done their A-levels, gone to university and ended up with important positions.

Children without the necessary abilities were practically forced to get an education they weren't suited to and often ended up with big problems. Many family tragedies unfolded as a result of the often well-meaning but misguided ambitions parents had on behalf of their children.

The worst examples of this, the ambitions of parents for their children within sports, I personally witnessed later on.

I was reminded of this the other day, during a conversation with our local golf pro.

We had just finished a golfing event organized by the Spanish Golf Federation with participants in the so-called "Juvenil" class, from 8 to 16, of both sexes.

He just shook his head in despair at how he had seen various examples of over ambitious parents dominating these children and youngsters during practice, resulting in both tears and the gnashing of teeth.

My own examples are similar when it comes to both tennis and skiing and from the time when my daughters were growing up and were, of course, members of the local clubs for these sporting activities.

This was in Oslo in Norway and took place on the so-called better west-side where we lived.

One could at times witness literally horrific incidents. I even had to cancel my daughters' memberships at the local tennis club due to its over ambitious leadership. The example is too grotesque to mention, but didn't directly involve my daughters.

It was not uncommon to see parents who, during simple slalom competitions, threw themselves out onto the slope, when one of their hopefuls fell, with an outburst of excuses that they had wrongly waxed the skis or that the fall had been caused by badly sharpened steel edges.

That one wants to see ones descendants be successful is obviously human, but with this type of ambition it backfires all too often.

Margaret Thatcher was buried yesterday, the 17th of April, 2013. Fortunately it was largely a worthy event where even the Queen herself was present.

The Iron Lady was both hated and loved, but as the first and only female prime minister in Britain, she must have had her ambitions under control.

A word on its own can plough better than the plough itself.
GM

Communication

April 2013

Communication is largely what one wants it to be. The communication I'm thinking of here is verbal. The best definition of communication is in my opinion "the process which has the unit of thought as its aim", from Wikipedia.

There are a large number of definitions, of course, just think of how versatile communication is, regardless of context.

As mentioned before, I'm married to Marianne who is Swiss. In May we will have been married for fifteen years and while my Spanish is quite limited, she speaks it fluently. I don't speak, which is her mother tongue. We have always, between the two of us, communicated in English.

(Even though I'm a British citizen, I've been based in Norway all of my life and have thus only my Norwegian school English as a starting point, and there wasn't a lot of regular school.)

Regardless, it's a great combination. Even though one becomes more tolerant and understanding towards one's marital partner as the years go by, very few believe me when I say that we in these nearly fifteen years have never come close to having what I would describe as an argument.

The answer lies, among others, in having as a safety net the fact that one isn't communicating in one's mother tongue. "I must have misunderstood what you meant", this immediately shows one's tolerance but also affords the better half the possibility of smoothing things over by saying: "Yes, I realise that you must have misunderstood, what I really meant was . . . ". Is this communication? Regardless, no one has to feel defeated or lose their pride; aren't we lucky?

I hope no one takes me too literally in this, it's probably not all that simple.

I don't think a poor foundation can be fixed this way.

Communication has, as mentioned, an infinite range.

Among current affairs there's the relationship between North and South Korea, or perhaps better put, between the two fractions, those who are tolerant towards North Korea's attitudes and those who belong to the other camp.

How far should one's tolerance stretch, seeing it all as a game playing to the gallery? Not only has the North lately caused major damage in South Korea as well as being responsible for a great number of lives being lost, but their threats are raining down in a way, which makes it difficult to understand.

Even outsiders like me understand that the masses, in a regime like the one found in the North, have to be kept under control and that the best way to divert attention from their own personal situation is to create a united front by showing outward strength.

Where then does communication enter the picture? Diplomacy should be tried to the utmost degree whenever possible.

But can diplomacy in this context bring results and is it at all possible to achieve a dialogue with a regime like that?

Apparently both Russia and China have finally admitted that North Korea has gone a bit too far. This could mean that the rest of the world is more or less united against what is happening, but then what?

Does one get a dialogue going because of it, and if so with whom, in order to find a solution?

The motivation behind the attitudes of the various parties in this conflict is not so interesting, but that China, and probably Russia too, see a united USA inspired Korea as a threat to the East, is not unknown.

"Communicare" in Latin; the process which has the uniting of thought as its aim".

Not that one should give up on it, but here it seems almost on a par with believing in Father Christmas, or isn't it?

Unity of thought - I would probably give up on in this conflict if I were involved.

By diplomacy one understands something to do with compromise, doesn't one?

Then there's something about not losing face. In some cultures this is probably the most important of all. To what extent this enters into things over there, I don't know, but it's probably an important factor.

We're talking about an autocracy, after all, and not a very enlightened one at that.

Can communication lead to compromise and, if so, what should it consist of?

One party cancels all sanctions and offers infinite financial support while the other promises to get rid of all its nuclear weapons and to shelve all further missile development. Is Father Christmas up and about again?

Think about the responsibility of communication.

Theoretically and only theoretically; had this last idea been put on the table as realistic, could it have been carried out without either of the parties losing face, and in this case, losing face to whom, the world?

Think about the responsibility of communication. What's the difference between Iran and North Korea when it comes to nuclear weapons and attitudes? In my opinion, it's just a question of time.

During the Cuban crisis in 1962, when we were closer to a nuclear war than ever before or since, the crisis was resolved by Khrushchev being given the opportunity to remove his nuclear installations from Cuba without their being bombed, while the USA committed themselves to not attacking Cuba and to removing its medium-range missiles from Turkey and Italy.

From what I've read I understood that Khrushchev at the time sent two letters within a short period of time. The first with the hope that the conflict could be solved through communication, while the second received a few hours later, had a far harsher content and a requirement which the USA in no way could accept.

Kennedy responded to the first letter only and ignored the second one completely. In his reply the opportunity, as already mentioned, was given to withdraw all installations from Cuba without any US bombing, which Khrushchev as we know accepted.

Thus, through communication and strategy, a catastrophe was avoided.

My personal experience with communication over the years has been all enveloping, in the sense that I as employer had had close contact with employees on all levels and of both sexes. Only rarely, as far as I recall, was it necessary to admit to a failure of communication.

I didn't always live up to the policy of my firm. Each employee should have full right to know as much about the running of the firm, so that even if they didn't always agree with its decisions and objectives, they should, if interested, be able to understand the motives behind them.

It obviously didn't sound quite like that in the company policy which I wrote at the time, but this part has unfortunately been lost somewhere along the way.

These days such ideals may sound totally misplaced in the business world and attitudes like these probably find little acceptance in today's personnel management.

In a family context my experiences as regards communication, especially in my younger days, were a little different. I was at times accused of being a coward when I didn't enter into what were, in my opinion, one-way arguments, the outcome of which had already been decided before any communication began.

There's something in the saying that "where there is nothing, even the Emperor has lost his rights".

Fortunately these situations were few and far between, but they stuck in my mind.

Distortion of the truth or a totally one-sided attitude makes communication difficult, if not impossible, and the same goes for unwarranted accusations. Desperation builds and that's when one sees compromise or giving up as the only solution.

Many will probably draw the conclusion here that I can't have been easy to get on with, and I can sympathise with this view. I don't my personal experiences have left scars that are too deep, but the wounds haven't been easy to heal.

I hasten to say that I have an excellent relationship with my half-siblings and my own close family, so in that context I'm talking about water under the bridge.

If a partnership is based on a solid foundation, it should in most cases be possible through communication to come to an agreement, based on compromise.

The way you look at beauty is reflected by your inner spirit.
GM

Compromise

March 2013

Everyone has a fairly clear idea of what the word compromise means.

Making compromises in our daily lives is quite common for most of us. We don't normally give it much thought nor do we look at compromise as being a sacrifice.

I give a little here, the other party gives a little there, then we make a compromise having given way more or less equally, without either party having got things exactly his or her way.

When travelling around, one has been places where in certain situations all trade is based on bargaining. The seller starts with prices that are sky-high, the idea being that these will be brought down to a level which both parties are happy with. This is also a form of compromise, but in my opinion a somewhat misguided one. Here there is no equal distribution of giving. The seller's contribution, the reduction in price, has been put in as a calculating factor. He knows where to draw the line, in other words, the lowest acceptable price, which still gives him a reasonable profit. The buyer on his or her part should also be aware of the situation and closes the deal only if he or she finds the price acceptable. Am I in the wrong here? I'm far from happy with this procedure, regardless of the cultures practising it.

If I have to compromise, however, perhaps it isn't so bad after all? Is it only because I'm generally not happy with this type of procedure that I don't like it?

Many of you probably feel that this is just the right form for trade, as here one can argue and negotiate and influence the final outcome.

At least that's what one thinks, but those of us who are a bit wiser, know that it, the price that is, has already been decided beforehand, it's the seller who decides.

Those who share my attitude normally pay too much, to the seller's delight. In other words, one ought to stay away from this type of trade if one isn't familiar with this form of bargaining. Some love it, they feel great when they can let loose in this type of situation and that's good for them.

Now, let's get back to compromise, which is the result of negotiations where none of the parties gets things 100% as they want them, but are still happy.

I mentioned that there is no sacrifice in this form of compromise and I actually believe that, but let's look at the kind of compromise where the distribution of benefits in no way is equal, where one of the parties feels that he or she has given a lot more that the other one, but goes along with it in any case. This can after a while be tiring. That it happens once in a while can't be avoided and it usually works both ways, but when the scales keep tipping in one direction it can become difficult.

In politics one can probably say that compromise is an obligatory factor, and here I'm thinking of the sort of politics practised in democracies and not those of dictatorships. Imagine how simple, there one doesn't have to think about compromise at all.

I don't intend to get into politics as such at this point, but just imagine if one had invented an enlightened autocracy. An autocracy which functioned exactly as it should, where social concerns were appreciated in a just manner, where human rights were accepted as the norm and where a perfectly run healthcare system benefited everyone. Fortunately I don't believe in this type of system either, but it would have been ideal, wouldn't it?

Otherwise I've always found that the model based on trust politics has many benefits. My uncle, Sjur Lindebrække, who was chairman of the Conservative Party from 1962 to 1970, wrote the book, "Faith and Trust" which I believe many of you might enjoy reading. It's not very thick, perhaps because its subject isn't very wide-ranging.

I suppose that I, in my more mature years, have come to the conclusion that this model isn't very practical to implement either. Here there's a question of too many compromises and we humans are unfortunately far from ideal.

Political coalitions are very much a question of compromise. Such mergers seldom make for dynamic governments.

In my opinion they are a bad use of compromise.

My original name, before I on my eighteenth birthday was given the surname, Manus, by my stepfather, Max, was George Hans Bernardes.

George after my English father and Hans because my mother felt there should be something Norwegian in my name. (Hans isn't just the name of a king of Norway from 1483, like George in England, but also a family name from Ulvik in Hardanger.)

Here there probably also was a compromise, as I was given the name, Manus, but was never adopted.

Enough said, the reason I'm going into details, is because I want to make a confession. Firstly, my father's ancestors apparently came from the Spanish Armada. Via Scotland under the name of Bernardi, ancestors by the name Bernardes appear in London in the 1800s.

I, myself, haven't done any family research but my sisters on my English father's side of the family have told me that, Artur da Silva Bernardes, president of Brazil from 1922 to 1926, was directly related and that my father's picture looks very much like him. Anyway, one doesn't have to look too closely into what sort of politics his party practised, it probably doesn't fit too well with our so-called modern world. Where they were concerned I believe there was no question of compromise.

The female president of Argentina, Kirchner, made direct contact with the newly elected Pope, Francisco, who as we know is also Argentinian, and asked him for his support in the debate about the Maldives or, as we normally call them, the Falkland Islands. From what I understand, the Pope strongly refused to get involved, which is a good thing.

Not that it will influence world development, but I've got a lot of sympathy for the way he conducts himself and for what I have understood about his ideals.

This seems to tell more about what kind of person Mrs Kirchner is and as one can probably understand, I haven't got a lot of respect for her. Thanks to the Pope's attitude there was fortunately no talk of any further compromise.

In relationships compromises are at times not to be avoided. This is fine as long as the partners are well-balanced when it comes to give and take. If there's a shift of balance it becomes difficult to maintain.

Compromise is a good thing, but make sure the balance remains constant.

Conscience

November 2012

Let me point out straight away that this is a very sensitive subject.

Conscience is probably one of the most flexible concepts there is as it always involves morals as well as judgement and feelings.

Everyone bases their conscience on their own judgement and ethics thus emphasizing its flexibility. In my book "Thoughts", the first 51 days of 2001, I wrote among other things about conscience:

"I suppose conscience is something we are all concerned about. Whether it be good conscience or bad, it will always be there as part of our daily life. Then there is something about suppressing a bad conscience and the pleasant feeling one gets from a good one. It may have to do with important things or just silly little things, but it is always on our conscience".

At that time, I meant it the way I wrote it, that everyone in one way or another is concerned about their conscience. Now, almost 12 years later, I've revised things a bit as one will see later, when I state that many seem not to have any conscience at all.

We have laws, of course, which in our democracies at least, are meant to be guidelines for how we are to behave in practically all situations. They are there for our own good according to those who have written them, but even though this is largely correct, I think most of us feel that we are swamped with laws and regulations and that many of them can only be understood by a selected few.

Everyday rules and regulations are fine, for example those concerning traffic.

Here it's a question of saving lives and reducing damages.

Every one of us decides how the state's rules are to be followed based on judgement and conscience.

After many years' experience of driving in Spain, my judgement is usually based on the theory that despite the speed limit of 40 most people drive between 60 and 80. The motorway limit of 120 means a minimum of 130 and is often closer to 150 with many exceptions over 170.

The stop signs mean, to a lot of people, just go if the road is free.

Especially in small towns the one way signs to most of the locals say " just go if no one is coming the other way and you can get to your destination quicker."

A widespread sport for those who normally drive at 150 on the motorway is to see how close one can get to the car in front without actually making physical contact.

I have to admit though that a greater respect is shown at pedestrian crossings.

It's no longer a sport to see how close to the pedestrians one can get without hitting them.

Most things are improving after all.

All aforementioned examples seem to be based more on judgement than conscience.

According to their own judgement everyone acts correctly.

That was all about judgement, but where does conscience enter into the picture?

Lots of people probably have no conscience at all, so they just drive around in their own world. While many probably have a conscience it's buried and doesn't surface until an accident has happened and it's too late.

For whom or for what should one have conscience in traffic?

I don't want to be seen as a saint in this case, because I'm not, but let's look at drinking and driving for instance. In this I'm quite consistent and I can confirm that since I was 20 years old and until I first came to Spain about 15 or 20 years ago, there was seldom, if ever, a question of having a single glass when the car was my method of transport.

Things did change to a certain degree upon arriving in Spain, where a glass or two with meals followed by a brandy with one's coffee, hasn't stopped anyone from driving home.

Having a morning coffee in the local bar, one often saw the local police with their "cajarillos", coffee with a dash of brandy, at the start of their working day. I think I think became quite conscious of what I was doing, drove more carefully and did not suffer from a bad conscience, but I would be telling a lie if I said that I at the beginning and until the late nineties, when I was here only on sporadic visits, kept to my Norwegian habits.

Gradually, as the rules were sharpened here as well, with regular controls, everything changed. Today the combination of drinking and driving has become unthinkable for most people and that's as it should be.

I don't know whether it has to do with one's conscience or one's moral responsibility not to hurt others, but if it has to do with both so much better, I now choose total abstinence when driving.

Perhaps most of it does have to do with the tiny good or bad consciences. The big ones are probably so overwhelming that if one has a conscience to begin with, one tries "the ostrich game". Puts one's head in the sand and pretends they aren't there.

Has anyone tried to examine or count their good and bad consciences? I wonder if one could come up with some sort of norm showing what percentage of either one would be within acceptable limits.

It would probably be too complicated, however, and one's conscience shouldn't be left to others as it is clearly among one's most personal possessions.

I have at least one bad conscience which I don't want to share with anyone until one day I've left it behind.

The more I think about all this, the more I have to admit that I too, to some extent, participate in "the ostrich game" in this context.

Conscience, judgement and moral belong together.

Of all the proverbs I've seen about the conscience, this Persian one is the finest.

"The zest for life comes from a clear conscience".

To paper

When one puts to paper what one thinks and means -
it can be interpreted wrongly and lead to scenes.
GM

Consequences
March 2014

The word consequence in itself says very little. The word can be used in many contexts, one of them being to bear the consequences of one's actions.

In my speech at the confirmation of my grandson, Nicolas, in September 2013, I touched on the theme consequences and that there are, for me, three stages of consequences, related to one's actions, all of which count in the development of human beings.

I quote some excerpts from the speech given on the 7th of August, 2013:

"First there is unconscious consequence.

That's the one all children instinctively use in their development. How far can I toe the line before I overstep it, that is to say, before there are unpleasant consequences? You have throughout the years been a very frequent user of this method, Nicolas, and it seems at times, that you cross the line with the clear idea that it'll be exciting for you to see what will happen next.

This procedure is, as I've said, used by all children and is a healthy one, although it might at times be a trial for the parents.

The next one is conscious consequence.

All actions have consequences in one form or other. As time goes by one learns, however, what the consequences of one's actions will be, though one often goes ahead anyway. One obviously learns from it, even though it at times can result in a black eye or maybe worse.

One also learns that consequences are not always the same each time even though there is the same sort of action. So this may result in new and surprising experiences. It takes time to learn this possibility, which can also be costly.

If one never risk an unhappy consequence, one would think that one would get away with it, but then one lags behind when it comes to experience and that may delay the process of growing up. To find some middle way would be my advice in this case.

The third one is a governing consequence.

That's the one where one before acting, carefully considers the consequences.

The action doesn't take place until one has a clear idea of its consequences.

When one has reached this stage, one decides whether the action is worth its consequences and is thus well equipped for one's further journey through life".

One can easily become confused if one looks more closely at what is really meant by the word consequence.

One encyclopaedia defines consequence as a logical follow up to a prior action. This can be a fact arrived at empirically or logically or an event-related reason for it to happen. One action may easily have several consequences.

Take a closer look at this explanation of a consequence and see if it becomes clear to you; I myself am having a bit of a problem with it.

Enough said, Nicolas at least seemed to think that he had understood its meaning. I can't imagine that he paid attention to the empirical or logical aspects of it; the word consequence is just something one understands intuitively, even at an early age.

The word empirical comes from the Greek "empiri", which in turn means "experience related". Not that I think you didn't already know it, but I looked it up just in case. As for the logical part, there's no need for further comment.

As for Nicolas, I believe he has a fairly strong "empirical" reason for his understanding of consequences.

One of the consequences of having a big mouth might be that one gets hit on the head. No reason to conceal that this has happened to me a few times, but it was in my early adolescence, long before I had a clear idea about consequences.

The older one gets, the more experience and the better equipped one is to analyse the consequences of one's actions, but one probably never manages to avoid all the bad ones. Neither does one necessarily wish to avoid all consequences, as there are also positive ones from time to time, which one wants to experience.

Oh yes, there are good consequences lying in wait all the time, even though the word consequence is used most often in unhappy circumstances.

An example of a good consequence might be that one has done a favour for someone which for the person concerned has been significant.

The consequence then is that one gets a good feeling, which is often worth much more than any other type of reward.

If one thinks about it, there are many actions in one's everyday life which can lead to good consequences, not least among people who are close to one another. A little attention, which often costs nothing, can result in incredibly good consequences. But, be aware, an unintentional word at the wrong time can lead to unintentional consequences.

At the end of last year, my wife and I undertook an action which was to have significant consequences.

I grew up with dogs and had, up until I married my present wife, at least one English setter. As a consequence of this, I believe in all modesty to possess a certain amount of experience when it comes to dogs. My wife had a short-haired dachshund for many years before we met each other, more than twenty years ago, so she also knows what it means to have a dog. Anyway, as a consequence of acquiring her last dog already grown, after a divorce had prevented the previous owner keeping it, it was both housebroken and well behaved, so she had no experience with puppies. And to make everything clear, I must also add it has been more than twenty years since I had my last English setter.

On my wife's initiative, after having talked it over for some time, weighing the pros against the cons, we decided in late autumn last year to check into the possibility of acquiring a little short-haired dachshund. I should add that dog number two during my first marriage was a compromise. As it wasn't too easy to have a hunting dog in a flat, we decided on a ruff-haired dachshund. I wasn't going to use it for hunting purposes, as I only shot birds during my hunting days.

As a consequence of having ordered it, the day came when the owner of the local pet shop in Vera, our nearest town, informed us that our short-haired dachshund "Duke", as it was already called by the breeder, was on its way from Toledo.

Since we at that point in time happened to be in Portugal playing golf, he consequently offered to keep it at his place for the week it would take us to get back.

All was well and the day of the big event came, when we went to pick up our new four-month-old family member.

The pet shop owner already had a French bulldog about four years old and when we met the two at the shop, it was clear that little Duke had already gained some respect. The owner told us that the little puppy from the very first day, had made it clear who got to eat first. The consequence of Duke's behaviour was that the French bulldog had immediately accepted the situation.

At the same time as we picked up Duke, my wife bought a lot of necessary equipment, such as a transport crate for travels complete with blanket, a bed to be placed in our little office, where we had decided the dog would sleep, a collar, a dog leash, fastening devices for car transport and some nappy-like rugs for the liquid and more solid stuff, which forms a natural part of every-day life. Furthermore there was food, treats and some toys for encouragement, with and without a built-in squeaking noise. The excitement was great and Duke passed water from pure pleasure every time we tried to pick him up.

The car had been equipped with a colourful plaid blanket, which we'd bought in Scotland earlier in the year and which we thought it would be good for it to get used to in the car.

Back home in the flat Duke immediately settled in.

Another Scottish blanket was put on one of the sofas, the one my wife normally uses, as we thought that's where the dog should stay when all three of us were at home and it felt the need to rest.

A couple of the nappy-like blankets were placed on the floor while our new family member inspected each centimetre of the office, passageway and the open kitchen section of the sitting room as well as the sitting room itself.

As a consequence of its short legs, it couldn't get onto the sofa on its own, so each time it tried to do this, it was lifted up. No sooner was it up there, however, before it jumped down again and disappeared into the office, immediately returning with one of its toys in its mouth. And so it went, non-stop, until it was completely exhausted. Finally it was sleeping like a baby until a short time later it was again going full speed.

On its travels it was sometimes out of our sight and as a consequence of our not being able to see it, it took the opportunity to do its business.
The rugs meant for this purpose were, of course, bone dry.

To make a long story short, all that was left to do was to put it in its bed in the office, turn out the light and shut the door. As it was clear that Duke was my wife's dog, as we all know there can only be one boss, she was the one to carry out the procedure. The big question, of course, was how it would react to it.

To our great surprise, no sound was heard from him until well after seven the next morning. Then, however, there was a lot of activity going on in the office.

We heard whining and tiny whimpers, and claws scratching the door. It turned out to be not the door to the passage and freedom that was being attacked but the cupboard door hiding the dry dog food.

We had closely followed the instructions for meting out meals, but already after just a few days of it showing constant hunger, the consequence was a slight upward adjustment of the food quantities.

The same ritual took place each morning. My wife in slippers and house-coat, collar and plastic bag at the ready, following behind a tail-wagging Duke, hoping that it would do its business outside. Unfortunately, a hope was usually all it was, in which case it didn't take many minutes from the time they got back in until it proudly showed us how clever it was, but seldom on the intended rugs.

The door leading to our bathroom and bedroom we had at first decided to keep shut. Everything inside there was to be out of bounds for Duke. After a bit of back and forth, using both one's index finger and a stern voice, it was also OK to leave the door open, so long as it could see one of us inside, but as soon as we went from the passageway into the bathroom or bedroom, it naturally became too much. Seconds later it was on its way in. The consequence being that the door remained closed most of the time. There are limits to what one can expect from a puppy, after all.

The greatest consequence of all in this case came after four weeks of having the most beautiful little puppy in the world. Practical experience and common sense told us that we were simply too "mature" to deal with the consequences resulting from having to raise a new family member and changing the life style we had become used to after fifteen years.

My wife brought the matter up with the owner of the pet shop one day when she was passing by. He told her that both his wife and daughter had been very sad when they had to give Duke away after the week he'd been there, but for obvious reason they had said nothing about it to us.

He said they had already become very fond of it.

As a consequence of this, my wife asked him if he would consider taking over the responsibility for Duke. He straight away consulted his family, who immediately and with great enthusiasm looked forward to the new addition to his family.

When I say that everyone was looking forward to it, I can't vouch for the French member of the family, but have since been told that they live together beautifully.

The somewhat sad consequence for us at the moment is the loss of Duke after the four weeks we had together.

The positive consequence is that we can visit it whenever we like and we experience the joy of seeing that it's not only got a good home but also another dog as a friend - even if it is a Frenchman who has quite clearly learnt to live with the consequences of having acquired a little brother.

Did you notice the great number of times I used the word consequences in this story? How many do you think there are? You guessed right, fifty-two times the word is mentioned.

So, as you can see, there is hardly a thing which, in some form or other, doesn't have consequences. I could easily have troubled the reader with more, but then this reflection would probably have had even more unintended consequences.

*If you don`t see it clearly at this point, you will one day understand that it`s through challenges that one learns and grows,
not so much while surfing downwind.*
GM

Curiosity
March 2013

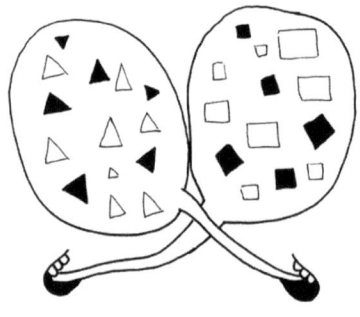

"I wonder what I will get to see, beyond the lofty mountains". Who wrote this I'm not quite certain, but I believe that it was the famous Norwegian writer Bjørnstjerne Bjørnson.

In my opinion it symbolizes curiosity. "The eye will surely meet nothing but snow".

Supposition, nothing certain, what else, curiosity.

Was it a quotation from Bjørnson or someone else, am I not curious about that?

Not really, I probably don't have the capacity to be curious about everything, that would be too time-consuming. There have to be priorities.

For the sake of this reflection, I had to check it anyway, and sure enough, it was Bjørnson. "Around and about there are nothing but trees, I would very much like to get across; - when will I ever dare?"

One would think after this that everyone has certain subjects for their curiosity.

If there is some truth in any of this, we're all curious, but for most of us our curiosity is limited to that which we feel strongly about or are especially interested in. In other words, the interesting question is not whether one is curious or not, as everyone is curious to some extent or other.

Does this mean that if one doesn't have the ability to ask questions, or is indifferent to finding answers to one's questions or if one hasn't got any questions at all, then one is lacking in curiosity?

Probably yes, but again, most people find, within their areas of interest, ways of showing their curiosity and thus find answers to their questions.

There's nothing wrong in that, we don't all have to be the same.

In my case, curiosity is the same as being and feeling alive.

I see it as a driving force, that which makes you put one foot in front of the other in your everyday life.

Curiosity is the driving force behind progress.

Forget the curiosity which makes one poke one's nose into other people's business, that seldom leads to anything good and one is better off without such information.

It's the curiosity which asks questions beginning with "why?" which in my opinion is the important one.

Again, when one doesn't ask questions one remains single-minded, one comes to a halt and doesn't get any further. It's good that I've come to the conclusion that we all have degrees of curiosity.

In November 1994 I wrote the reflection "Why?" When I refer to events during my time at school in Italy as a 17-18 year-old, I wasn't as aware of things as I became later in life. That's why I asked questions like: "What makes us so often ask the question, "Why?". Is it because we're curious or because we're ignorant?"

I saw "why?" from a completely different angle then than I did later on, but perhaps it helped me become aware of the word as I understand it today.

My angle then had more to do with language and communication than with the more general significance of curiosity as the driving force behind progress.

Can one be curious about curiosity, or is that gilding the lily? Does one in that case end up in a never ending circle? If one is curious about something, without having found the answer, one can, of course, assume an answer and renew one's curiosity on that basis.

I've always been into technical challenges and have in all modesty found solutions to various such challenges. As one can see, I prefer to call them challenges instead of problems, and these solutions have led to both patents and the manufacture of new products.

The expression "problems" is negative, whereas the word "challenges" trigger solutions.

This sidestepping is another matter altogether but I'm convinced that everyone who has had anything to do with product development will agree with me that in order to find satisfaction in this field one has to be curious and look at "why?" from the above-mentioned angle.

Curiosity is the driving force behind progress.

I'm curious as to whether anyone has got anything sensible out of this, but

I'm not really interested enough to ask. It could result in my having a set-back which would reduce my curiosity and, as one may have understood, I would rather not lose it.

About having regrets

I regret very little of what I have done
as luckily my memory's quickly gone.
I regret more what I didn't get done,
all of which would have been second to none.
Gave people a chance – from near and far,
always kept the door ajar.
Yes, it has often been very dear
and hasn't always got out of low gear.
A tougher stand with demands and decision -
would that have been the way to greater expansion?
Undoubtedly short term but therein lies the strength,
of those who know their profession at length.
One needs practical experience and time to roost,
maturity, effort and lots of boost..
GM

Dependence

December 2013

In some form or other we are, I believe, at all times and throughout all stages of life dependent on someone or something. From the time we see the light of day for the first time, we are dependent.

No sooner has the umbilical cord been cut than we are normally at the mercy of the person we have been dependent on throughout the entire pregnancy, the big difference being that now others can move in and help take over some responsibility for our further development.

Regardless, we are still at the mercy of and dependent on someone else.

No matter where in the world we happen to be born, and under whatever circumstances, rich or poor, those who think money makes one independent are terribly mistaken; we are always dependent.

Can't one make oneself independent from dependence? Only by extreme manoeuvres I would think. But does one really want to?

Dependence is quite natural, has a completely natural place in one's everyday life.

We are always learning something, whether it be part of our formal school education or not.

Also, when after school we get out into the real world, it is always a question of learning something.

The day one gives up and says enough is enough, there's no point in learning any more, that's really the beginning of the end.

We are, regardless of how we look at it, dependent on others in order to learn.

It is said that he or she is self-taught. The basis of being self-taught must start with something one has learnt and thus, if one look at it in isolation, it is probably more a case of indirectly building on the experiences of others, which reveals us dependent again.

Dependence as a challenge faces a large number of people who for various reasons need others around them in order to exist.

I can imagine, even if it isn't part of my own experience, that most people in such a situation will do their utmost to become independent.

Unfortunately certain situations often make this impossible; one just is and always will be dependent on others.

The above examples relate to human dependence. What about the more distant dependences, those most of us don't think about too much in our daily lives?

For those of us who are lucky enough to be growing up in the so-called modern world, it is natural for both clean water and electricity to be present at all times. We take it for granted and complain about the smallest inconvenience caused by a power failure, or having no water for a few hours when a pipe has sprung a leak. Here we have entered into material dependence and this comes in many guises. We, the spoiled ones, take too many things for granted; after all, we pay for them through our taxes, don't we?

On the screen, appeals are made to put aside a few kroner a month for those millions of people who don't know what clean water looks like and who barely come into contact with electricity in their everyday lives. Some people must go along with these requests or we wouldn't see such campaigns on TV.

There are pictures of children drinking water with which we wouldn't even mix cement and they have to walk for hours every day to get to water sources for these precious drops. Regardless of our social level, dependence exists.

We have also become totally dependent on mobiles and the internet, as well as an ocean of other gadgets and we feel that the world is coming to an end when occasional irregularities occur with these. We obviously are happy to be dependent.

Indeed we insist on it in our everyday lives by always aspiring to the newest and latest gimmicks. This, of course, doesn't apply to everyone but clearly to most of us.

Another form of dependence, and one which can be more serious for the person or people concerned, is the dependence which can affect one's health or which often destroys family life. It is easy to say that here one has to be careful, as I believe there are several factors playing a part. Each and every one has to think about themselves and their own lives. Otherwise, to the extent one finds time and interest, everyone can choose to involve themselves in organizations they believes may have a positive influence when fighting dependence and abuse.

I myself have fortunately never got to know any form of what I, from lack of knowledge, lump together under the heading "drugs".

From the age of seventeen to twenty-three I smoked cigarettes. The reason I quit over night was that I throughout adolescence had a constant struggle with my tonsils. Finally the day came, when I was called in for an operation to have them removed. My innate fear for everything to do with hospitals and white coats spurred me into action. The hospital visit was cancelled and my last cigarette extinguished.

The fear must have remained in my subconscious, however, because until the last couple of decades I have at times had very unpleasant experiences with tonsillitis, but have never again smoked.

Alcohol is a different story. Despite a steady trickle of red wine throughout the years, from the time I first discovered this gift of Bacchus, during my two-year stay in Italy at the age of seventeen and eighteen until today I can honestly say that there have been no negative side-effects. I have since the first days of my youth never had what one might call a hangover or to my knowledge any other adverse effects. The volume has stayed steady and more or less at the same level for the last fifty years.

When my daughters grew up we constantly heard about tragedies happening as a result of one's becoming acquainted with certain types of "substances".

I believe I chose the easiest way out by making it clear to them that regardless of how much I loved them, I would help them with anything else, but if they got involved with "drugs", they would be on their own. I believed then and I still do, that this is something everyone has to deal with on their own. When one has got into this vicious circle, one can only get out of it on one's own. I'm humble and tolerant when it comes to other points of view in this matter, but I'm happy that we, as a family, have been spared this - at least as far as I know. Since I myself have never been a gambler, I also don't know anything about this dependence except what I can read about the problems which may befall both families and people who are unable to moderate themselves in this context. Again it's a question of personal balance and control over the danger of becoming dependent.

It seldom affects one's health where a balance exists but there is no doubt that many families have broken up and that related tragedies take place every day.

To use but not abuse, in other words to find the golden middle way, in all of life's challenges is what one ought to strive for; but never forget that one must also live the one and only life one has been given on earth to the full.

A smile is like sand on ice, it helps you walk more safely.
GM

Details

In many ways it's a pity that what counts are the details,
as they are often boring and time consuming to put into place.
GM

Experience

October 2013

There is something pretentious about the word experience. "Experience suggests that". As a general expression one normally lets it pass without closer reflection, but if it is connected to serious speeches presented by people in authority, one ought to listen carefully. Where would we be without the lessons experience teaches?

Wouldn't we just be repeating our actions, whether or not the repetition is justified?

How often would we be correct in our repetition? In our everyday life we are not consciously aware of the way we use our experience. For most of us, we automatically draw our own conclusions. We base our actions on our experiences and subconsciously make minor or major adjustments.

As a result it is one of the main factors which help us develop throughout our entire life. It would be very sad if we at some point told ourselves that that's sufficient experience, let's flick the switch.

In a way it would be the same as putting one's hands in the air saying that now I've got nothing more to learn, there's no point to the learning process.

Those people who consciously acquire knowledge until the very end are the happiest.

It is of course also true that theoretical knowledge also builds experience, though not immediately in a practical way.

Is there also something called spiritual experience which complements practical experience?

Through schools and universities one gets an academic education. The experiences one has gained as a result of one's studies are, of course, both valuable and necessary, one hopes, when it comes to applying for a job. But even when one's career choice isn't of a practical kind, but of a more academic type, the question of experience is always raised.

One stands there with one's exam results and is more or less treated the same as all the other applicants. Regardless of who gets the position and the criteria used, one can ask oneself who should cover the costs in order to get the experience which has to be gained to do the job properly.

It's most likely the employer who has to invest in order to benefit fully from their employees' education, and that is probably as it should be. Naturally enough one can't be equipped for the task one is given before one has gained the right experience.

A different situation involves education of a more basic character, which needs to be combined with business practice within a chosen profession. This combination of schooling and practical experience is in my opinion by far the best when it comes to career choices. I hope it still exists in some form or other.

At the time when I started working, at the end of the fifties, we had several apprentices employed in our firm. They were to reach their journeyman or trade examinations.

They were normally employed in the service department, had apprenticeship contracts and, if I remember correctly, were given two days a week off to attend the vocational school to get a theoretical education.

As far as I can understand, this arrangement has been replaced with other versions but I'm not up-to-date on this.

The question is if the apprenticeship scheme, in a more modernized form than the one we had back then, wouldn't be better and more interesting for many of those who feel the need to get into a craft early on, rather than fight their way through a higher theoretical education in which they have little or no interest.

I have heard that the apprenticeship scheme is practised successfully for instance in Switzerland and that in England there are constant references to the fact that more apprenticeships ought to be created.

I take this as a sign that this form of education is still considered the best when it comes to practical training.

I greatly believe in a working environment involving a combination of theoretical and practical training.

I have often heard i said. "If only others could learn from our hard-earned experiences, how much better everything would be." That way of thinking is both short-sighted and meaningless in my opinion. One has to be master of one's own experiences; I'll go as far as saying that it is only through one's own experiences that one can progress. Here I exclude obvious well-accepted experience based on investigation and science. Such experience belong to all theoretical education on all levels and automatically provides a positive benefit in most cases.

In this context it is clear that knowledge can be drawn from other people's experiences.

Not that one ought to believe that all experience is worthwhile, and I don't think anyone does. Everyone has, in one form or other, suffered a bad experience.

The conclusion is that it isn't really important if one's experiences are good or bad as long as one learns from them.

Bad experiences don't trigger repeats, while the good ones ought to do so..

I believe it would be good for us all to focus more on the value of experience.

Think about the experiences one has benefited from in life, especially where one believes they have been important for one's development. Then become more conscious of them.

Most of us are, I believe, equipped with a good or not so good ability to suppress bad experiences. I call this ability a safety valve.

We can't keep filling up with too much negativity, especially as regards the bad experiences we suffer from at times.

We ought to suppress some memories of them, when we feel that it is necessary, in order to maintain an acceptable balance.

The best experiences which have contributed to my development, I believe I gained during my time at school in Italy in nineteen fifty-six and seven.

Keep your eyes open and the journey will last longer.
GM

Feelings

April 2014

Everything in life must have to do with feelings. Without feelings mankind wouldn't have survived.

According to the encyclopaedia feelings are described among other things as emotions and affections. Emotions involve various complex mind reactions, such as pleasure, sympathy, compassion, sorrow, disgust, etc. This might become clearer if one uses the example that it is impossible to be happy on request. Feelings have to be real and immediate.

I feel that most of us have clear opinions about feelings.

We become acquainted with feelings from a very early age. Children show their feelings unconsciously and without reserve; they are wonderfully innocent.

Real feelings have to be separated from false ones. All of us probably feel intuitively what is meant by this.

Priority must here - as elsewhere in life - be given to honesty and then all of this becomes a lot easier. Apart from a few exceptions, which I don't see any reason to get into, there is no point in compromising, as it's only a question of time before one is found out, usually followed by unexpected and unpleasant consequences.

What would love be without feelings? The answer speaks for itself, doesn't it?

Real love can't exist without feelings and that means that love based on false feelings hasn't got anything to do with love. Strong opinion?

Absolutely, but as always just my opinion, as I am convinced that there are others who would put it differently; to each his own.

To show and express feelings is something very personal. In most cases, the ability to do so goes deep, but that doesn't mean that those who outwardly have difficulty showing or expressing their feelings lack the ability to do so, the opposite is often the case.

Trust and security may often be what's needed in order for introverts to open their feelings up.

Regardless, everything to do with feelings is a delicate balancing act which, if it doesn't happen naturally, is also not right.

To have feelings for someone is not the same as to feel for someone.

Compassion is a certain type of feeling which doesn't directly affect oneself. It's a feeling one gives to others in the form of sympathy and understanding.

If someone gives naturally to another, the good feeling returns like a boomerang which makes it feel especially good.

It's well-known that animals have senses which we humans don't share. It is said that they can feel earthquakes, storms and other natural phenomenon before they happen.

Because we humans feel that we have physical control over most things, we set aside the fact that we also possess senses of a special character. There's no doubt, in my opinion, that such senses were more prominent in pre-historic times, but as evolution changed us into more "modern" beings the need for these ancient senses diminished.

Nevertheless, there are still some remaining capabilities from the days when we were more "animal-like". Not everyone is aware of this and why should they be, as the need for them is no longer obvious in one's everyday life.

The expression "I feel it in my bones" is one that fits into this category and which sounds perhaps very grandma like.

Regardless, if you leave the door of your scepticism just slightly ajar, this isn't so far-fetched. Most of us haven't heard of it or perhaps even felt it.

Good feelings, mixed feelings or bad feelings. I think most of us can distinguish between these three types of feelings, that is to say, more precisely identify which one of the three applies in any particular situation. Why? Because one has a feeling about it, that's all.

Likewise I believe it to be easy for most of us to describe others as either not having any feelings or being cold or warm when it comes to showing them.

It becomes more difficult when it comes to describing oneself. I'm not quite clear on what it means "to listen to music with feeling". It probably doesn't refer to the music itself as having feeling, or does it? No, it's probably that one's feelings become engaged when one listens to certain pieces of music which makes one feel good.

Up to now it has all been about emotional feelings and the incredible sense they represent, if feelings can be characterized as a sense, that is.

What then about the physical side of things, the one which has to do with loosing one's feeling? The term is too broad to broach here, but in my opinion there is no doubt that those who, in some form or other, have experienced this have their own special challenges to deal with. Perhaps it's often because in such situations one chooses to keep one's feelings to oneself.

Don't you also feel that there's some truth in this?

After committing this reflection to paper, I seemed to remember that I in two previous reflections had come close to dealing with feelings and right enough, when I went through them I found one about "sensitive hands" from April 1994 and one on "sensitivity" from May of the same year. (REFLECTIONS I)

I have to admit that it would be too much for me at this point to check if there are any contradictions or repetitions present, but there must presumably be some sort of connection between sensitive hands, sensitivity and feelings.

Perhaps someone has sufficient energy to take a look?

Time

**It's not so important what time it is -
what's important is that it passes.
GM**

Human Development

April 2014

I don't suppose anything exists that doesn't have to do with development. Whether it be ourselves or others, we are always developing. What's the reason for our developing in different directions, if that's what we're doing, and why does it happen?

Without development I believe there is no future. Many people claim that we're developing too quickly and in a lot of ways I can understand that too.

Lots of people have problems keeping up with and dealing with the ever/ changing realities. I had a totally different view of this in my youth, of course, when development couldn't be quick enough. It was always about reaching something, whether it be age-related milestones with built-in rights, or goals set as part of one's own development.

With seventy-five years on the clock, I see things a bit differently today.

I find it good that there are fractions in society protesting against this and that. It is fine as long as it doesn't get fanatical. Once in a while we need to be reminded that we are all responsible for what is happening and that we often, at least to some degree, can accept our share of responsibility by taking action.

When we these days hear about the consequences which will follow what the experts see as inevitable, namely global warming, I often use the example with the Thames, the river which cuts London in half.

About a hundred years ago, the river was practically dead.

Not a single species of fish could survive in its contaminated water. The contamination was clearly caused by human beings and they were also the ones who pulled themselves together to do something about it. The river is long since back to "normal" with all its fish species present and everyone, or at least most people, seem to be satisfied with the result.

This is not to say that the problem with global warming is just as easily solved, but if it is so that it has happened as a result of human influence, it makes me believe that we in time can tackle this challenge as well.

In what way, no one knows and perhaps the following Danish proverb doesn't quite fit the bill here, but anyway: "Necessity teaches a naked woman to spin".

I'm convinced that I'm not alone in my changing views on development, that is to say the development to do with human beings which, according to the title, is the one I stick to in this reflection.

The kind of development which has to do with humans and their ability to adapt, I became aware of after I in 1983 for the first time arrived at the place which later has become the basis for my retirement years.

At the time, we belonged to the little village of Turre in the eastern part of Andalucia, in the south of Spain.

Turre is, even today, thirty years after I first set foot there, apparently relatively insignificant, as a quick look at the computer answer to a Turre question doesn't tell one anything of significance. It also has no special meaning for this example of development.

The first time I drove down its main street, which was indeed paved, there was little to show that "modern times" were approaching. What there was of shops and bars was presented largely by holes in its white walls.

Street lights had still not arrived and when one saw women outside it was almost always before dusk and then as usual dressed in black. Their daughters, who were also consistently dressed in black, were solidly rooted in the crook of their mothers' arms while the boys were given a freer rein, but not a lot.

Necessary information to the people, of whom at the time more than half were gypsies, was given via loudspeakers placed at strategic points throughout the village. Illiteracy was high among the adult portion of the inhabitants and everything to do with legal matters limped along on twos and fours.

Undoubtedly it was very charming, but the point I'm trying to make is that only a few years later, as more and more foreigners like myself found their way to sunny southern Europe, a radical upheaval took place among the locals. For hundreds of years most things in their lives had practically stood still. Even at the time when I arrived, donkeys were used to transport fruit and vegetables to the market.

Real estate which earlier had been worth practically nothing to those who didn't use it to grow things on, was in a very short time converted into gold mines.

The transformation over ten years was like night and day. Young people in bright coloured clothing went to the disco, there was no talk of staying in after sunset. Whether it be girls or boys, they raced along on scooters and even the mothers went through a change from a safe black to more colourful clothing. I'm not sure it's correct, but it was always said that one at the time could buy one's permits or what we call driving licences for cars.

Both women and men, who had previously barely ventured the ten kilometres down to the Mediterranean, were in ever-increasing numbers seen in large expensive four-wheel drive cars.

The male part of the population continued to do what they had always done in their daily lives, but the economic "liberation" meant that more and more bars and shops appeared.

I must hasten to say that not all were landowners, or had land which appealed to foreigners, but they all, in some way, went along with the flow of social change taking place. The fact that new jobs were created on a large scale within construction and its related subcontracting businesses, happened at the same time as a lot of new service type professions saw the light of day.

The building boom took off and banks and shops opened up in large numbers. This was the case until the first really big challenge at the beginning of the nineties. Then came a crash in the form of a sudden halt in development.

An international economic crisis followed by a standstill of practically the entire machinery. One soon got to feel what we in Norway among others have the following expression for: "After the sweet scratching comes the bitter burn".

Why then this little story? Well, because we have here witnessed such a radical development over so few years, that I dare say their "souls" have had problems keeping up.

The upheaval came too suddenly, the money too easily. That which in Norway took close to fifty years to put together, if one can say that it has been put together, happened here in less than a fifth of the time and this must have affected the people.

In this context one must also not forget that the dictator Francisco Franco greatly influenced this society from 1939 until he passed the reins to the son of Don Juan de Borbon, Conde de Barcelona, Juan Carlos, in 1975.

If these upheavals have harmed the population permanently, I don't know, of course, but I believe they to some extent have affected its mentality.

There is also something in the saying: "Time heals most wounds", so we'll have to wait and see, but the last big crisis will be felt and remembered for a long time to come.

Dear . . . , give me a chance
Give me a chance to love thee -
Give me a chance to be me -
Give me a chance.
Give me a chance to give thee and take thee -
Give me a chance to always have thee -
Give me a chance, please be so kind -
Give me a chance, I know thy mind.
GM

Ignorance
Oct. 2013

Why on earth am I dwelling on this word. Fortunately it isn't used all that much, but when it is, it's usually in a serious context. If it is so that we in our daily lives connect ignorance with stupidity, as I believe one does, then that's wrong, in which case it might be worthwhile immersing oneself a bit in ignorance.

I don't in any way wish to compete with Wikipedia or others who, in page after page, present all sorts of interpretations of the word. Perhaps I see something contradictory in the interpretations I'm dwelling on.

If ignorance has something to do with ignore, which sounds reasonable, it might seem a bit affected to say that to ignore means something like: "to refuse to take into account", whereas ignorance is described among other things as: "to pretend not to be aware of or know anything about this or that, or to be indifferent to".

If one looks at the word ignorant which must also have something to do with ignorance, then it is described, among other things, as: "to lack information about or knowledge of this and that". And in this context also: "to lack education or to be unsophisticated".

The word ignorant is further described as: "a person who is in a state of not being in the know; often used as an insult to describe those who ignore or discount important information or facts *on purpose*". I see this as being the same as: "to express oneself against better judgement".

It already becomes difficult for the average person to keep up and these are only a few simple approaches.

I would probably not have started grappling with ignorance if I hadn't had a few experiences of my own related to the word. These I won't refer to, neither with names or situations, but more with attitudes which I'm sure several people can identify with, either by doing a self-analysis or by examining their own experiences.

The ostrich is reputed to put its head in the sand when it senses danger.

It then is supposed to believes itself to be invisible and thus can't be noticed. The ostrich is claimed to believe it is less visible and therefore feels safer, so what then has the ostrich got to do with my experiences of ignorance?

Well, even well-educated people, who are in no way stupid, can in certain situations act with ignorance.

Complete information can be available in all aspects of a case. It is also known with reasonable certainty that the people concerned do have all the information.

External indoctrination probably also plays an important role when it comes to behaviour patterns.

It happens again and again, however, that behaviour pattern shows that actual, available information is completely set aside, in other words, ignored, a fact which invariably displays ignorance on part of those concerned, or does it?

Is this then deliberate, or does it just happen? Is it a form of possible protection, like the ostrich act, or is it a fully conscious act?

Again we must make clear that: "Ignorance differs from stupidity, though both can lead to unwise actions".

As far as my own experiences goes, I choose to believe that some actions haven't been fully conscious. Because when I choose to believe that the actions were deliberate, the whole thing takes on a more serious aspect, which might lead to much more serious consequences.

Good thing I'm tolerant.

In politics this type of ignorance occurs in everyday life. There actions are fully conscious. A politician knows that they are talking against their better judgement, as that is what is necessary at times; it is this which, in my opinion, is unfortunately part of politics. Can it be described as a form of dishonesty?

If I stick to the earlier description of the word ignorant: "a person who is in a state of not being in the know; often used as an insult to describe those who ignore or discount important information or facts", then it's the one I adhere to when it comes to my own experiences, and the aforementioned comments about politics.

Had one had an open world championships in the art of distorting facts, I believe Iraq's Minister of Information at the time of Saddam Hussein would have won the gold medal in 2003.

Muhammed Saeed al-Sahaf, popularly called "Chemical Ali", appeared on TV with comments like: "There are no Americans in Iraq, those are only illusions".

The Americans were at the time about 100 kilometres from Bagdad. He became a hero, with his own internet page. If it's true or not shall remain unsaid, but the Iraq papers claim that he committed suicide by hanging himself shortly afterwards.

Well, this was probably also a form of politics.

Knowing full well that I may have misunderstood some details in my interpretation of ignorance, I'm right, at least according to my own assumptions. If you're curious as to what I mean by that, you can take a look at one of my earlier reflections: "What is right and what is wrong?".

I have to admit, however, that even though I wasn't conscious of it, I may, in a pinch, have used this form of ignorance myself.

It wouldn't surprise me if to "express oneself against one's better judgement" is considerably more widespread that I've assumed.

Survival

For a lot of reasons I want to cry-
For a lot of reasons I call them a lie.
GM

Imagination and Creativity
March 2014

That I'm embarking on the imagination again, exactly one year after my first one, is purely due to an occupational hazard. Insufficient order in my PC and a brain which can't keep up, have made me reflect on the imagination once more. I must have forgotten to erase the heading from my list after the first one was written.

My subconscious seems to be very concerned with and focused on the imagination, but that it's possible to attack it again now, without being able to recall that the same subject was dealt with a year ago, can't be a good sign.

Instead of calling them Imagination 1 and 2, I separate them, referring to them as "Imagination and Product Development" and "Imagination and Creativity" respectively.

As regards the imagination, it is probably here as in many other contexts so that we humans have been equipped with different amounts.

Whether imagination is an ability which can be measured, I don't know, but my observations tell me, at least, that we have all been equipped to a greater or lesser degree with this incredibly important capability.

Even though we all probably believe that we understand the meaning of imagination, the word comes from the Latin "imaginatio" and it is explained as the ability to picture the unknown, the not present or the non-existent.

It probably would have been no good if we had all been equipped with a full tank of this ingredient.

A reasonable amount of imagination, however, I believe helps stabilize us, we need it in our daily life if we don't want it to become too stereotyped and dull.

Imagination and dreams, do they go hand in hand? I guess we can't really decide what to dream, can we? The dreams just come as they come and when they come.

This applies, of course, only to the dreams we have when we're asleep. Completely different is what we associate with daydreams, because they are normally conjured up in a conscious state. In daydreams there is usually something negative from society's point of view. This because the daydreamer seems distant, not present; that's just it, one consciously directs one's thoughts towards areas completely different from those which are currently relevant.

Enough said about dreams, they'll be dealt with separately.

One's imagination, however, is something which one to a certain extent can control oneself, that is if one is fortunate enough from the start to have been given a pinch of this.

The expression to imagine things may not seem very serious to most people.

"He or she is always imagining things". But can't there be something creative in it?

"Use your imagination" is a frequently used expression. Does it mean that one is given free rein to improvise and to use unconventional methods to solve a challenge or to achieve something?

It sounds creative, but the prerequisite is, of course, that the person using his or her imagination has the ability to do so.

Some people are, in my opinion, totally lacking in imagination, it's almost as if they can never get their thoughts off the beaten track and that makes it all far too difficult.

Not necessarily for them, as they have a narrower view of the case in question, in other words, a view devoid of imagination.

Then there are those who, given the task of "using their imagination", spontaneously think that here there's an opportunity to be untraditional, thus choosing procedures outside acceptable methods. Does this mean that "using one's imagination" in certain contexts requires a certain responsibility?

The answer is undoubtedly "yes", again in my opinion.

I'm always using "in my opinion" because I clearly see here as elsewhere that others may have entirely divergent views on the matter.

I have observed that someone I definitely believe to have imagination, suppresses this. Can it be fear of stepping off the so-called beaten track? Does one think one can avoid challenges by curbing one's imagination?

Anyway, if someone feels comfortable doing that, that's fine, we are fortunately all different.

It's difficult not to involve creativity when thinking about the imagination. It feels as though the two go hand in hand, as if imagination is needed in order to create. If the same applies the other way around, I question; that is if creativity requires imagination.

About the imagination it is said among other things that it differs from creativity by being "cognitive". Oh, well, that takes care of that, doesn't it? Then it shouldn't be difficult to keep the terms apart, should it?

This becomes even clearer when we see that the expression "cognitive" appears as the opposite of the emotional or intuitive and that it has to do with recognition, perception and thinking.

One thing said about creativity is that the ability has to do with knowledge within a certain area. Further it has to do with knowledge about creative processes, in other words different methods of innovation.

I hope that this is meaningful for you; I on the other hand just now have big problems accepting this and understanding that I, who have always considered myself as having both imagination and a reasonable degree of creativity, will have to slacken my sails and perhaps stop imagining that I have both.

If I continue to use my imagination creatively my way, however, something positive may one day result.

Mini prayer

Dear God my utmost thanks to <u>you</u>
as you're the best, they are your due.
GM

In all Honesty

September 2012

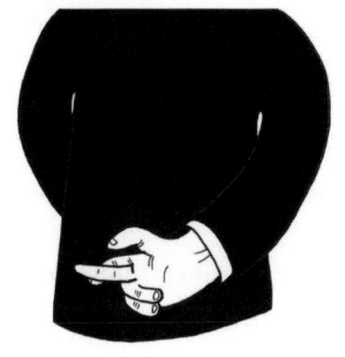

It is high time I grabbed hold of "honesty" and finally came to terms with this, for me, painful subject. Ever since I started working I have been immensely irritated over the expression, "to be honest", or its other variation, "in all honesty". Not only has it irritated me all these years, but at times also made me furious, because a more idiotic expression, in the contexts it is normally used, I cannot envisage.

How can one trust someone using these kinds of phrases? What the person in question is saying is that normally I am a totally dishonest person, but in this particular situation I will make an exception, namely to be honest. Stuff and nonsense.

Now, of course, there will be many reading this who, if being honest with themselves, will realize that they themselves use this expression.

To you I have only got one thing to say, and that is: stop using it this very instant.

Next time you hear a politician expressing him- or herself, listen carefully. You will be surprised at how much dishonesty you will observe. This, of course, is not only related to politicians.

Of course, one can only say that this does not mean much in the greater context, as it is only a matter of expression. In no way can I personally take that attitude.

While I am on the subject, it feels natural to add the expression: "Truth be told". What on earth is the meaning of that? Should the truth not normally be in the forefront?

Does it mean that one is not normally trustworthy, not expressing the truth? Is the truth to be saved and only brought forth at special events or occasions?

In my opinion, if that is the case, the world has become unhinged.

A typical old-man's expression you might say. Very well, but if that is your attitude it means that you are either indifferent to the above-mentioned approach, or you accept it.

Do not forget that another generation is coming after us. What are they going to believe and think if we don't give them guidelines?

Again the excuse of many will be these are just cliches.

I regret this attitude is to prolific in our daily communication. Most of us, I think, will fight for the freedom of speech and the right to express ourselves. In the spirit of democracy we want it that way.

Some Danes have made cartoons offending the Prophet Mohammed, while a video recently produced also seems to offend those who worship the Prophet, and who have him as their guide in life. Retaliations, riots and killings have been the result of it all.

We live in a world which allows us insight into whatever we want. The whole world is open to us if we are interested.

How many religions and communities do we have on this planet? Furthermore, how many sects and special varieties do we have who represent different opinions of how life should be lived and what it should consist of.

At the end of the day the question will be and has probably always been the same, who is the strongest, who will win and what means will they use in order to win, or at least advance in the hierarchy of preferred religions and their splinter groups?

However, "being honest", I think that every one of us should be able to live as we wish and make the best out of our life on earth, based on our own assumptions, but that is when I am "being honest".

This last statement has probably got its weaknesses.

What would I mean in this context if I were to be dishonest? If I had skipped the first "to be honest", I think my basic attitude would be crystal clear.

Summary; I think that every one of us should be able to live as we wish and make the best out of our life on earth, based on our own assumptions.

Intuition

May 2013

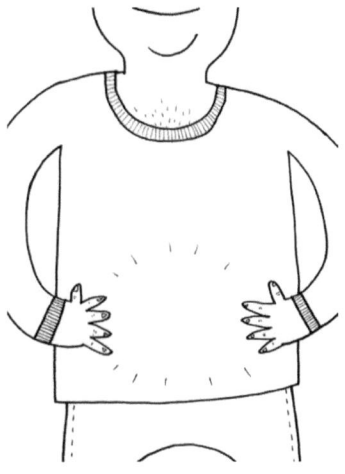

Everyone has probably some experience with what we call intuition. That most of us perceive what is meant by intuition differently, is only natural, what's important is that we are aware of it, that we can sense something which we don't quite understand. It just happens when it happens, without any prior warning. Intuition is, among other things, described as a feeling – a sudden understanding or sensation of a case or situation. It mustn't be confused with instinct, which is understood to be the logical connection between a challenge and its solution.

It's important to notice the described difference between intuition and instinct.

If we stick to the explanation of it being something which we don't quite understand, it becomes easier.

For me, a clear example of intuition, is something which happened many years ago, at the beginning of the eighties.

My then common-law wife and I had spent a lovely holiday with my cousin and her husband on Tobago in the Caribbean.

It was January and it was a holiday which I will never forget.

I had had minimal contact with my cousin as we were growing up, apart from a period just after the war, and thus can't say that we knew each other well.

My common-law wife, if I remember correctly, had only met her on one special occasion at one of my mother's so-called "round" birthdays. That's when we agreed to go on this holiday.

The trip itself and our agreements have no bearing on the matter, except to say that we had an unusually happy time together and that my common-law wife and my cousin got on especially well. To what extent the contact was maintained I don't remember, as they lived in Bergen and we lived in Oslo, but I believe there was rarely any physical contact apart from special family occasions.

I don't remember if anything unusual took place before it happened, but one night my common-law wife had a terrible time without much sleep. She had a nightmare without her being able to explain what she had dreamt, but she was sure something terrible had happened. I seem to recall that she woke up shortly after midnight and that we both had trouble going back to sleep.

Just before eight o'clock in the morning the phone rang. Slightly confused, I answered and immediately recognized my cousin's husband's voice.

Unable to express himself very clearly, he tells me that my cousin died in the night, just shortly after midnight.

Who got the greatest shock I don't remember, but I think it must have been me. She, after all, had been pre-warned that something terrible had happened and was in a way prepared for it.

It's important to listen to female intuition. I doubt that the person exists who hasn't heard about it.

How can it be that women seemingly not only have more intuition than men but a more accurate version as well, or is this just hearsay?

As I now enter my think tank and search my memory in order to find some examples of my own intuition, it's almost hard to believe that I can't find any.

I ask my wife, who immediately answers that she believes she has quite a few, but the concrete examples must be buried deep because she can't seem to come up with any either.

I'll have to try again later and see if I can't put some down on paper by tomorrow.

It could simply be that I also have several examples of my own intuition, but that they're stored in a drawer difficult to open, we'll have to wait and see.

I've suddenly remembered something which might be relevant to intuition: In management and seen from a commercial angle, (where one doesn't, as in the example of my then common-law wife, look at an event directly after having had a dream) I feel my personal experience stresses that intuition has been more important to me than many other management tools. It isn't the case, of course, that intuition should be allowed total domination, but in many contexts, it has been the so-called "gut feeling" which for me in the final analysis has been the deciding factor while when making decisions. After all, this expression is more or less synonymous with intuition, isn't it?

Now we're starting to get a bit more meat on the bone in my opinion, at least when it comes to understanding.

Some people go so far as to say that intuition is a sort of sixth sense. I believe, however, that one has to take care not to isolate intuition and thus place it on a pedestal. On its own and without support, intuition as a management tool becomes somewhat dubious. I'd prefer to see it in association with personal abilities which over time have been built up and shown to be predominately useful. Is this what's called experience? Regardless, it's unwise to underestimate experience.

The word "vardøger" in Scandinavian folklore, describes a sort of accompanying spirit which precedes the person it's connected with by letting itself be heard or seen just before the person in question appears. It is described by some as a premonition – one experiences or feels something before it actually happens.

What made me bring "vardøger" into this just as it was starting to look simple?

Again, intuition is described as an immediate understanding or feeling in any given case or situation. A "vardøger" as a warning spirit preceding the person it is attached to, to be heard and seen just before he or she appears.

I have difficulties making clear distinctions here, it's a bit like walking on a knife edge in my opinion, but then I'm no academic.

Just before the telephone rings, one knows that it's going to ring and even who's ringing.

This we've all experienced – is it intuition or "vardøger"? If I had to make a choice here, I'd say that it has to do with "vardøger", but I'm far from sure of my decision. What is clear to me, however, is that when intuition is used as a management tool, as mentioned above, then there is no comparison. Imagine if one were to make "vardøger" part of business transactions?

I realize that I'm in deep water here, so I'll have to see if I can pry a few examples of female intuition out of my wife. I tried to yesterday, as I've already mentioned, but without succeeding, we'll have to see what happens.

My intuition tells me that she's working on it and that I, some time or other, will be given not only one but several examples.

Laughter
April 2014

That a good laugh prolongs life, I firmly believe. Having the ability to laugh is a privilege. Whether it be stories that are told or films that one sees which trigger the laughter is of no importance, the important thing is that one laughs. Nothing is as liberating as a good laugh.

Even though it isn't scientifically proven that laughter prolongs life, a fit of laughter feels good.

Not everyone laughs at the same jokes or the same comedians. These funny men or women appeal to us in different ways. When it comes to comedians, we all have our favourites, and it is fortunately so, here as in all matters, that we're not all the same. My observation is that there are more men than women in this humorous category, but that might even itself out over time, as so much else, mightn't it?

Some like the simple and crude forms of humour, while others see the comical in more complicated forms and yet others enjoy the whole range.

There are many who react negatively to the crude form of humour. It is simply too primitive. Could the reason be that if they laugh at it, they reveal their own primitiveness?

I myself believe that I have a reasonably well-developed sense of humour, spanning a fairly wide range, in other words; the simple and crude can at times be wonderful, but the more complicated ones also make me laugh.

In my opinion, Rowan Atkinson and John Cleese cover quite a wide range and I seldom miss an opportunity to see them in action on the screen.

The BBC has always been a leader when it comes to humorous series of all kinds. Once I have caught on, they seem to become timeless.

Earlier on, at home in Norway, when all is said and done, Fleksnes was probably the one who could most easily get the laughter going.

For many, a comedian is someone who can tell jokes. That interpretation is for me too simple. In my opinion it's often difficult to separate the individual as a provider of humour from the series themselves, in all the various programmes made by the BBC throughout the years. I stick to the BBC as that's where I watch most of these kinds of series. One thing is certain, however, if one doesn't understand the language and its nuances, it's impossible to derive full pleasure from them.

Here it might be tempting to mention several big names, but I'll let each of the readers search their memories for some of their favourites.

That in itself might bring on the laughter.

Apropos of watching funny programs on television, there is something which especially irritates my wife. Not that they are the types of programs she appreciates the most, but whenever she indulges in one, the canned laughter irritates her.

In many ways I agree with her, it's as if we need a reminder of when to laugh. Oughtn't this to be left up to each and every one of us?

Many of these programs are, of course, recorded live in a studio with an audience, but even then it seems like the laughter and applause have been orchestrated.

Anyway, this is an individual matter and perhaps the programs would seem totally different if one self and one's nearest and dearest TV watchers were the only audience.

Laughter is, among other things, described as producing sounds as a reaction to something funny. That ought to mean that there are many shades of laughter.

We're all familiar with the giggling and tittering which often form part of whispering and murmuring.

What the difference is between chuckling and laughing, I am not sure, but we understand it anyway, the same as when some guffaw while others chortle. These expressions may not be used that often, but we know what they mean when we experience them.

Those who have experienced a fit of hysterical laughter probably don't forget it too easily.

In that state, there's more to it than just producing sounds, one's entire body is often involved and one needs a large portion of self-control in order to stop oneself. Even though one, after repeated sobbing, appears to have reached the end, new outburst often follow. Normally one feels exhausted after such a séance, which is often based on virtually nothing.

Is laughing the opposite of crying or the other way around? I certainly believe so; it's all about expressing feelings, to express happiness or sorrow. When someone cries, we feel for them, and this is a completely natural reaction, which doesn't necessarily mean that we immediately start crying with them, even though that also happens. When someone else laughs, we aren't automatically asked to laugh along with them. If one for instance is a group listening to a joke being told and hear the others laugh, one isn't necessarily expected to laugh along for politeness sake.

It is entirely up to oneself. We fortunately react to and perceive things differently.

It also happens that one hears others laugh even though one sees that they haven't really understood the joke. That reaction is somewhat special, but if one is observant one can see that it happens.

To be laughed at is for many a hurtful matter, but it is a weapon which is often used.

Since laughter is normally released as a reaction to humour and there is something called gallows humour, why isn't there something called gallows laughter? Oh well, such questions one can ask if one wants to put things bluntly or is a bit twisted.

The expression "it almost makes me laugh" one often hears in reference to something meant to have a bit of self-irony.

"It almost makes me laugh when I think of how stupid I was not to have piano lessons". "It almost makes me laugh when I think of the times I've regretted my choice of club after having made a golf swing".

This is not an expression I myself normally use, but I still ask how the laughter comes into it and why one almost has to laugh. If one almost has to laugh, then one doesn't really laugh, does one? It is as if something has to be added in order to give it meaning. The expression is also used without the word almost and then it all takes on a bit more meaning, as one actually laughs, but then again, why does one laugh at for instance not having had piano lessons. It can't really be a laughing matter, can it?

And what about sarcastic laughter? It is also one of the less amusing laughter's, which nevertheless, like being laughed at, is often used as a weapon.

For me, the "artists" who make us laugh deserve great respect and that it is a form of art, I don't doubt for a moment.

Dear God give us a chance

Give us a chance, for what we want and pray -
Give us a chance, so we don't lose our way -
Give us a chance.
Give us a chance, please tell us what to do -
Give us a chance, we know we want to -
Give us a chance, if you so please -
Give us a chance, we will manage with ease -
Give us a chance.
GM

Looking out for number one
October 2013

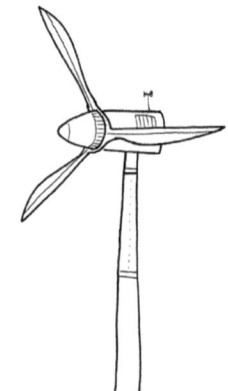

Nothing can make one reach one's boiling point more easily than fanaticism.

People fight for their ideas and rightfully so. However we humans have a habit of not always agreeing. That is also good, as many different points of view can create a broader understanding; provided, of course, on whether one is not fanatically concerned about one's own perception being the only valid one.

Let us in this context disregard fanaticism.

Isn't it easy just to sit on the side-lines with one's opinion when a challenge is raised? No problem, the matter has nothing to do with me, at least not directly, it lies somehow outside one's perspective, one's hearing or a number of other senses.

Oh yes, from that standpoint it is easy to have an opinion, even a solid opinion of the matter. It's easy to find arguments for and against when one is sitting on the side-lines, knowing that one isn't or won't be affected by it. In such a situation it's easy to simply be objective.

Imagine, for instance, how important renewable energy is.

With renewable energy I believe one means energy taken from sources which have a continuous supply, as for instance hydro power, solar energy and wind power.

Spain is one of the most developed countries when it comes to wind power. In 2012 sixteen per cent of the total electricity consumption came from wind power. When one drives along the coastal road from Algeciras in Andalucia, near Gibraltar toward Cadiz, one soon passes Tarifa with its hundreds of wind mills or more correctly put, wind turbines.

Wind mills were, as we know, used for other things than the production of power at the time of its invention, a long, long time before electricity. There is hardly an area in Spain nowadays where one doesn't see these enormous three-bladed monsters rotate. All well and good, as one just drives by these areas after all and the type of energy produced is just fine; none of us wants the temperature of our planet to break the thermometers.

In the mid-nineties, a request was received by the municipal council of the village our urbanization, Cabrera, belongs to and where we were living at the time. Turre is its name.

Whether the request came from a private company or from the government is uninteresting, but there was a question of getting permission to install a series of wind turbines on the mountain above the urbanization. The municipal council found the idea interesting at first and went ahead with hearings and other forms of investigation.

There was, of course, an outcry in the urbanization, not least was the argument that it would make property values go down radically, it was used to its utmost. It ended at that time, as luck would have it, with a dismissal and up to now we have been spared seeing a single turbine in the area. But we are, of course, all agreed that renewable sources of energy are important, aren't we?

Only a year after this episode a small delegation of military representatives appeared on the scene.

They carried maps and range-finders and had started drawing a route through the urbanization. Here pylons would be installed for an electricity cable to be strung up to a future radar station on top of the mountain.

Who had sent a report to my wife about the delegation being in the area shall remain unsaid, and it is also of no interest, but it didn't take many minutes before she was in full confrontation with its leader. Where was the permit to appear in her area and who was responsible? To make a long story short, it ended with her engaging the sharpest lawyer in the area and "digging her trenches". No problem getting a hundred per cent of the households behind her.

I choose to believe that it was her resolute reaction and engagement of the lawyer which resulted in the plans being put on ice, but I realize that if they had had an overall plan which they wanted to implement, there would be a radar station on top of the mountain today, but perhaps with its power supply outside the urbanization. If there had been a question of having brought the cables up from the other side of the mountain, it would, of course, have been perfectly OK with us, even though it would probably have passed through dozens of other properties.

We wouldn't have been affected, after all.

It is now about seven years since we moved away from Cabrera. We're living at the thirteenth hole of the golf course in the urbanization, Valle del Este, a bit less than half an hour's drive from Cabrera, but as one can see, in the same area. We no longer belong to Turre, but to the town of Vera, a town of about ten thousand inhabitants, five minutes away from home by car.

During this period the Railway authority has started and partially completed important stretches of a fast line for the so-called AVE between Alicante and Almeria. It concerns a high velocity train connection which, via Murcia, will bring travellers from Almeria to Madrid in about three hours. I would be surprised if we live long enough to see this, but one never knows what will happen.

At the moment the whole thing has been postponed due to lack of financing. There are, of course, an infinite amount of houses and properties affected by this, but when we're sitting at our local restaurant by the golf course enjoying a simple tapa with its traditional glass of wine, looking towards the town of Garrucha, down by the Mediterranean about 10 kilometres away, we can barely see the train line. Far beyond hearing and almost out of sight, we are fortunately not affected. Perhaps one day, higher powers willing, we will be able to see the snake speeding past at almost 300 kilometres an hour, before stopping a bit farther east at the station in Vera. We're lucky as there is normally a greater distances between stations.

If we get to experience this scenario at all, it will probably be long after we have already handed in our driving licences and we will be driven by taxi the few kilometres to the station for a week-end trip to Madrid.

It is, of course, wonderful to think that we can't be anything but positively affected by this innovation, if we are affected at all, that's to say, if we manage to take part in the event.

High velocity trains are in my opinion an excellent form of communication and if we are lucky enough, that is to say, if all goes according to plan, a station in the area, certainly means that property prices will be secure when the economic situation improves.

But again, one must obviously be sorry for those who are directly and negatively affected by it, but I reckon those who feel they can stop the development are few and far between.

I understand Spain to be one of the most advanced European countries when it comes to the development of high velocity trains and that one should, of course, be happy about.

In the above I have stuck to the more collective aspects of "looking out for number one" for the good reason that it can easily become very personal. It is probable that everyone can come up with a number of examples of how we all look out for number one, but that's up to each and every one of us to dwell on, that is if one has the courage and wish to do so.

Just don't let it become a burden on your conscience, as that normally has enough to worry about.

Physical strength alone doesn't necessarily mean that one has drawn the longest straw.
GM

Negligence
March 2013

This will probably become more like a report of an event, an event which for me has been the most challenging I have ever experienced. Names and related documentation are of no interest at this point, the complete report and the documentation pertaining to it will probably later be presented to the appropriate authorities in Norway. I'd like to point out straight away that I haven't in any way got the necessary credentials to assess the qualification of doctors, so when I ask myself questions regarding the subject it is pure speculation.

I go back a few years in time and start by pointing out that I as a married pensioner live in the South of Spain. My wife is from Switzerland and has lived down here for about forty years.

She speaks and writes Spanish perfectly and I can, among other things, thank her for the fact that everything seems to have ended well. None of the doctors in Spain spoke English and since my Spanish is seemingly rusty, most of the communication took place through my wife.

Most of my adult life, I have had annual medical check-ups and have in the main had good health.

Apart from pills against high blood pressure and somewhat reduced hearing in my right ear, I consider myself being in good shape for my age as I approach seventy-four. I admit to having reached the repair stage, which implies that I no longer feels everything to be as before and that I subconsciously am prepared for health problems to appear.

I became a member of Adeslas, a private Spanish health insurance company in 2007.

This happened because my wife throughout the years has been a member of a similar scheme and we at the time saw quite clearly that it might not be so good if we belonged to different schemes, in other words, with me in social security and my wife in private healthcare. Having different doctors and hospitals would easily become a challenge.

Let it be said immediately, I have only heard good things about Spanish Healthcare in general, whether it be Social Security or Private.

Because I still visit Norway a couple of times a year, I have, despite my membership of Adeslas, had my annual check-ups in Oslo, at a medical centre, which, as far as I know, is well-renowned. This has been happening for years.

An appointment is made at more or less the same time every year, the check-up is done and the results are obtained by phoning the nurse about a week later. In the latter years I've been told to keep my prostate under observation.

I requested early on that extra checks be made regarding this if possible, as I have several friends who have had unpleasantness and operations in this respect.

Here I must add that in all the years since my eldest daughter died of cancer in 1990, visits to the doctor have generally been a challenge for me. My nerves are on edge when my blood pressure has to be taken.

My last check-up was done in August last year, in other words in 2012.

I called for the results as usual a week later. The nurse told me everything was fine but that the prostate still had to be kept under observation.

I can't remember why but I asked her to send me the results through the post. The envelope arrived and was filed away by my wife. I've never looked at them and have no idea about what levels they should be. I assume that everything's OK and all I have to do is to wait for next time.

On November 22, 2012 a letter arrives from the doctor in Norway, saying that he has been   waiting for a phone call.

In the letter, which also contains the last four years of test results, he asks me to drop by in the next few months, so that we can check and follow up the prostate issue. He points out that there has been an increase in the PSA (prostate level).

Instead of planning a trip to Norway in January – February, we decide, mainly on my wife's initiative, to contact a doctor down here.

An appointment was made with the first urologist in the Adeslas list on December the 13th. The woman doctor works at the Virgen del Mar hospital in Almeria, just an hour's drive from home.

We gave her the test results for the last 4 years, 2009 – 2012, which she quickly looks through.

After having shaken her head several times, she says that if I had been her patient, I would have been called in at least two years ago.

We're sent to the Adeslas offices in Almeria to obtain an authorization for a biopsy, return the same day to the hospital and are given an appointment straight away with a male doctor who is to do the test. He turns out to be a surgeon, and the one who would do the operation should it become necessary.

All the tests were done in rapid succession, and two days later, on December the 15th, the surgeon himself did the biopsy.

I suspect he already knew it was urgent, though he never said so.

We spent the night before at a hotel in Almeria as the biopsy was to take place early in the morning.

We weren't summoned to another meeting with the doctor until the 17th of January as it had taken longer to get the biopsy results due to Christmas.

The doctor explained that a tumour had been found in the prostate and that an operation should take place as soon as possible. He explained that the operation was a category 6 one, but he expected it to go well.

Preparations were made for the operation, my lungs were x-rayed, a blood test was done and an electrocardiogram was performed the following day, January 18th.

On January 24th we delivered the results of all the tests to the same doctor, who ascertained that all the tests were in order and that I was ready for the operation.

On January 29th the doctor himself called with the message that the operation would take place on Friday the 8th of February.

There was something about the delay being caused by the anaesthetist himself having become ill and having had an operation himself.

On February 7th we went again to Adeslas in Almeria to obtain an authorization for the operation.

We stayed the night at the Grand Hotel and were at the hospital at 8 am the next day.

The operation took place at 9:30 am. It lasted three hours and we were later told that the tumour was bigger than they thought at first, but that the operation had gone well.

I woke up in the operating theatre and was wheeled to the recovery room.

After a while I was visited by my wife, who was relieved after having talked to the doctor and been told that the operation had been successful.

The type of operation is in Spanish called: "Prostatectomia radical ampliada, Linfadenectomia Ureterocele".

Around 8 pm I was moved to a private room where my wife was waiting.

Equipped with a catheter and various types of drips, we spent the next 5 days being given wonderful care and visits from the surgeon each day.

He was very happy with the way things were going and on the 13th we were able to leave the hospital.

The period from the 13th until the next visit with the doctor on February 21st was mainly spent in bed under my wife's loving care.

The next appointment with the doctor took place at 2 pm on February 21st.

The result of the operation was in and we were given to understand that it had been touch and go. There was something about the result being a three and had it been a four it would have been very bad.

The 23 stitches were removed and we returned home.

Another visit to the hospital followed on March 4th. This time the catheter was removed in the operating theatre, by the same surgeon as before and my return to a more or less normal life began.

A few days later the surgeon phoned, asked how I felt and told us to make an appointment with him after Easter for an ultrasound.

An appointment was made for April 4th at 8:10 pm.

We arrived with time to spare and were let in at 8 o'clock. After two minutes he stated that everything was fine. A pleasant conversation and confirmation that I was in the clear followed, with a request to return in June to check the PSA level. A fantastic personal follow-up from start to finish.

On the 14th of June another blood test was done. The result was picked up on the 18th, followed by a meeting with the doctor on the same day.

He stated that the PSA level was down to 0,030 ng/mL and that he didn't think there would be any further negative results. My next check-up would take place in December, six months later.

Knowing what I had been through during this period, being unsure of the outcome and dependent on others, I couldn't help being frightened.

Are the rules different from country to country or is it a matter of one's qualifications not being sufficient?

It'll be interesting to see what they say about the matter in Norway, if there are different warning signals there, if there might have been some medical negligence or if it's a question of lack of judgement.

Maturity

Arms that are wrinkled and knees that are bent
who has you their intimate friendship lent?
Is it what one sees and what one smells
which really one's true story tells?
One can hide the rest, but not the best -
it always appears with zest.
It's what we stand for and what we go for,
which defines us for ever more.
GM

Nicolas' Confirmation Speech

August 2013

Dear Nicolas,

That you of your own free will wished to be confirmed, I found to be a very good decision. The law which made confirmation compulsory was passed in 1736 but rescinded in 1912, so for the last 101 years everyone has been able to choose freely.

Two years ago, in my confirmation speech to Oscar, I covered most of what I felt should be said at this time and I'm thus having trouble finding new things to say.

Regardless, most of us see confirmation as the transition into adulthood and that has to be the most important aspect, if one isn't more deeply involved in religion. How you feel about that, Nicolas, you may keep to yourself.

Anyway, my advice about letting the Word of God accompany you throughout life, is not bad, and just as I passed it on to Oscar, I now pass it on to you.

During your preparation for today you have probably gained a complete understanding of what the word confirmation means - both to reinforce and confirm, and what it entails.

Well then, Nicolas, what about the transition from childhood into adulthood? That this is what confirmation symbolizes you have obviously known for a long time, but what might not be completely clear to you, is that the transition doesn't happen from one day to the next and that is something you have to both accept and prepare yourself for.

In this context, I would like to give you a few words to think about along the way.

At first, something simple about the word tolerance.

It means among other things, to tolerate, to be able to stand something, but not in the sense of physical strength. Tolerance is the ability to tolerate, in other words, to be able to live with those whose opinions, attitudes and actions are different from and unacceptable to oneself. The meaning of this word can serve as food for thought for all.

Then about the word consequence. It can be seen in many different contexts, but the short version has to do with accepting the consequences of one's actions.

For me, there are 3 stages of consequences which count when it comes to human development and the transition from childhood to adulthood in particular.

First there is the unconscious consequence.

That's the one children instinctively use in their development. How far can I stretch the line before I overstep it, in other words, before it causes the wrong sort of consequences.

You have over the years been an especially frequent user of this method, Nicolas, and it seems at times as though you overstep the line with the clear idea that it will be exciting to see what the consequences will be.

This procedure is, as I've already mentioned, used by all children and it is both natural and healthy, even though at times it can be quite an ordeal for the parents.

Number two is the conscious consequence.

You perceive that all your actions lead to consequences in one form or other and you learn to understand what the consequences of your actions will be; despite this you go ahead. You probably learn from it, even though it can hurt at times, even result in a black eye or something worse.

Furthermore, you learn that the consequences are not always the same for the same type of actions, and that can lead to new and surprising experiences.

All this it takes time to learn, which again may be costly.

If you don't act at all, you might think that you'd get away with it, but the consequence of this is that you lag behind when it comes to experience, which in its turn can delay the process.

Staying somewhere middle-of-the-road would be my advice to you in this case.

This is the stage you're at today, Nicolas.

Third on the list is the governing consequence.

That's the one where you carefully consider all possible consequences before acting. No action takes place before you have a clear idea of its consequences.

Once you get there, you decide, before taking action, if it's worth the consequences. Only then will you make good progress in life.

As you can see, Nicolas, even though this short version of consequences probably seem complicated enough, we're talking about a gradual transition and it's you yourself who always decide how long the transition will take. You decide through your daily behaviour and attitude, how and when the various stages of your transition into adulthood will be reached.

For some the transition period from childhood to adulthood lasts a long time, whereas for others it goes quickly.

The most important element is that the transition be as right for you as possible, not that it be as short as possible.

Whether you like it or not, Nicolas, your mother and father will be the judges of your development during this period. You naturally won't agree with many of their decisions, but that you have to learn to live with.

All decisions they make on your behalf, they make with love and with only one thought in their heads, that it will be in your best interest.

It is often hard to swallow that that's the way things are, but you will gradually gain a greater understanding and hopefully also a greater tolerance.

It is this, among other things, which characterizes your move into adulthood.

Don't forget that you also get good support from your godparents.

You can also be proud of having a big brother like Oscar, though I won't go into that here. Don't ever forget that blood is thicker than water.

If you don't yet see it clearly, you will one day understand that it is through challenges that one learns and grows, not so much when one is surfing down wind.

Even though you've had easy access to a lot of things, you've already had your challenges and up to now, it looks like you've handled them well. There are no limits to what you can do, Nicolas. Focus on what you want to achieve and think back to a time when you've already achieved what you had fought for. Go with the feeling and ask yourself if the result was the way you'd expected it to be. If you're not happy with it, there's no shame in turning back or trying a different direction.

The recipe for a happy life no one can give you, it is once again up to you.

You alone make the decision, you cannot blame others.

Be curious about life, be curious about everything, ask questions, be active and don't let the world go by without getting involved.

Seize the opportunities when they appear, use but don't misuse them.

Be open, remember that nothing enters a closed hand and that pride goes before a fall.

Smile even though it doesn't always come easy. Be polite and attentive and don't forget the importance of being a good listener.

Learn languages and use them to get insight into other cultures.

Behave towards others they way you expect them to behave towards you.

Be aware of your responsibilities in all situations but, at the same time, don't forget that you also have your own life to live.

With this advice as part of your rules in life, you should be well-equipped, Nicolas, to meet the world which lies at your feet.

Granny and I love you a lot and I'm proud to be your "Bappi".

A toast from all of us to wish you all the best, Nicolas.

Oslo 7.8.2013

One always has a choice – there's nothing odious in that - but certain standards for oneself must be set.
GM

Opinions

April 2014

If you haven't got an opinion about anything at all, you are, in my opinion, seemingly lost. Most of us, however, have opinions about most things, but having opinions isn't worth much if one doesn't know how to express them.

To have opinions and to be able to express them if one so wishes is, at least in those democracies I'm familiar with, a privilege worth fighting for.

It is a human right which should never be taken for granted. We have all seen tragic examples of suppressed freedom of expression.

No debate on my part about freedom of expression, it ought to be taken for granted in an enlightened world, the way I see it, but unfortunately that's not the case everywhere. Even though there is freedom of expression, it isn't necessarily so that when one has an opinion about something, one must express it, put things bluntly or fight on the barricades for same.

Another thing is that to keep certain opinions to oneself, is a piece of advice I would like to give to all those who have a tendency to spill over with them.

I actually don't believe that so-called normal people exist who don't have opinions about anything at all, everyone probably has opinions, it's part of the pulse of life.

On the other hand, those who have so-called convictions are perhaps few and far between. Anyway, as I've said, one doesn't need to fight for all one's opinions, but when one has so-called hobby horses, understood to mean things one feels strongly about, then it's good to have convictions. It means that one stands by one's opinions and fights for them.

Here one has to, as in so many other contexts, be aware of the challenges connected to what many of us see as fanatical opinions and attitudes; but that's a totally different matter.

Fanaticism we'll put to one side in this case, it is scary enough in itself, as we've seen many examples of. It, fanaticism, is unfortunately everywhere, in all social, political and religious fractions and exists in almost all contexts. There is no doubt that we, for ever or at least for as long as human beings rule our world, will become acquainted with this unpleasant evil, fanaticism.

In early adolescence it is normally so that many of us are concerned with choosing what is right, according to the opinion of others, for fear of being looked upon as outsiders. Human beings are, as far as I know, defined as "pack animals", in this case to be understood as having identical beliefs, it makes them feel secure.

As one gradually starts to feel comfortable with one's lives and more secure in oneself, most of us will form our own opinions about certain things which will differ from those of others.

This I believe is related to the interests one has or acquires, but it is proba-bly also a result of social and cultural influences. In many ways this is all well and good, as it is the fact that we aren't all the same, which adds spice to our respective lives.

We have something to compare with when we or, better put, if we are able to see our own opinions in relation to existing general norms.

Many great personalities throughout time have had firm opinions about almost everything, which I believe is both reasonable and correct, even though their opinions didn't always turn out to be the right ones, that's how it must be.

In order not to make it too close to our time, we can use an example which goes almost two thousand years back in time. The then Roman Senator, Cato the Elder, is said to have ended all his speeches in the Senate with the subse-quently famous sentence, here translated into English: "Furthermore I believe Carthage must be destroyed".

The reason for this was allegedly that he believed the city's wealth to be a threat to Rome.

Well, we can only hope that Cato the Younger, that is if he existed, learnt from this.

Firm collective opinions, virtually bordering on the fanatic, I myself have fought against without success. Whatever touch of diplomatic attitude I might have, immediately came up short, but a very special experience it became.

The time is the late eighties and the place is Cabrera, the urbanization in the South of Spain where I had just begun my long term plan to establish myself when my retirement age was invariably reached, if I managed to live that long, that was.

I had already made good contact with the establisher and developer of the place, a very charismatic English architect, a good fifteen years older than myself. His name was Peter Grosscurth.

Unrealistic laws, or perhaps the lack of same in Spain, were at that time, as far as I could understand, both unclear and flexible. A great deal of improvising was required in order to get the books to balance in this context and it didn't help that additions and changes took place continuously, with or without retroactive effect.

Enough said, the above mentioned Peter had on-going challenges with the inhabitants who had already established themselves in the urbanization, as to which of the various common expenses they had to bear, as well as a number of practical details to do with the development itself. Practically speaking, this meant that a lot of them didn't pay anything at all.

As extenuating circumstances for the implicated, one has to mention that language and communication problems, as well as an understanding of the legislation, played a part. One day as Peter and I sat talking about the problem, which to me seemed totally crazy, I proposed that I make an objective attempt at mediating in the conflict. A certain amount of experience in human relationships I believed myself to possess after some decades as leader of a fairly large family business.

The day came when I had gathered together thirty or forty of the protesting clan for an information meeting. Food and drink had been organized and the atmosphere was good from the start. Peter was obviously not there, so it was just me and all the rest.

I had prepared myself well, I thought, and had committed everything to paper in order that nothing be left to chance.

Everyone listened without any form for interruption and I felt that I had fairly good control of the situation.

I believe my speech lasted about ten minutes whereupon I opened for a discussion about the arguments.

A few questions, for the sake of understanding, were raised here and there and answered before I asked everyone to respect the laws referring to everyone having to share the communal expenses in order to secure the future value of their respective investments.

After a short time where one in groups had continued the discussion, one of them comes over to see me and says something like: "George, I speak on behalf of all of us. We largely agree with your argumentation and also that you have put your case well, but you can tell Peter from all of us that we won't pay anything at all before we are threatened by law to do so".

Neither before nor after have I heard such a collective opinion on something from so many different types of people.

What I didn't know at the time, however, but which later became clear to me, was that these people, who were mainly English, had previously been stationed in different countries around the world and had now settled here as pensioners. As the prices in Spain had already at this time made a great leap upwards, their economic situation had reached its breaking point.

In other words, it probably wasn't so much a lack of will as of possibility, and then it's of course important to maintain one's prestige.

It eventually ended up with many of the properties changing owners and what became of the hard core I don't really know, but I hope at least that the ones surviving, if any of them are still alive after some twenty-five years, are doing well.

The regulations came into place eventually, the urbanization was fully legalized and these days it's neither misunderstood laws nor the government's responsibility that one is still doing battle, but so it is.

People's divergent opinions based on their different views on most things, is in the final analysis the reason for the on-going challenges in this little oasis. Fractions are formed and contrary views are put to the test.

And for those of you who think this is an exception, in other words, that which has to do with divergent opinions, take a closer look with this in mind, and see if it isn't your opinion too, that this is reflected everywhere.

Oscar's Confirmation Speech

August 2011

Dear Oscar,

Today is your day and only yours. You yourself decided that you wanted to be confirmed and I believe it to be the right decision.

I hope it wasn't just the thought of the presents which lead you toward a Christian confirmation.

I myself chose not to be confirmed and thus don't know what depth the religious aspect entails, however, it can't hurt to have been through the process.

For most of us, situations occur from time to time, where having the Word of God to accompany us is not to be sneered at or, at least, where a prayer can be of comfort.

The shock we all felt on the 22nd of July makes it easy to understand.

Anyway, what probably isn't known to all of us, is that confirmation was made compulsory by law in Norway in 1736. If one hadn't been confirmed before the age of 19, one could be punished with both the workhouse and the pillory.

Additionally one wasn't allowed to do one's military service, get married, be godparents at a christening or testify in court without one's confirmation certificate.

This injunction remained in effect until 1912 when confirmation became voluntary and all penal laws were rescinded.

The word confirmation comes from the Latin "confirmare" and means to reinforce as well as confirm. Who confirms what, I believe varies according to the different religious groups, but since I don't know much about it, I won't dwell on it.

What's important is that most of us see confirmation as the transition from childhood into adulthood and that's good.

There's only one catch to this, Oscar, and that is that you won't suddenly be grown-up as of tomorrow, even though you might wish to be.

We're talking about a gradual transition here and you yourself get to decide how long this transition will last.

You yourself decide through your daily behaviour and attitude, how and when the different stages of transition are achieved.

Your "judges" will be your mum and dad, with whom you won't always agree. In other words, it won't be different from the way it has always been. This is, however, quite ordinary and normal.

What you in future will become more and more conscious of is that you, at the different junctions in life, will gain an ever-increasing understanding of why your "judges" decide as they do. All, absolutely all the decisions the "judges" make, they make with love and with only one thought in their heads, that it will be in your best interest. You might see it differently and it can, of course, happen that they on hopefully rare occasions judge wrongly, but you will gradually gain a greater understanding. We have all been through this process.

That's what shows that you're growing into adulthood.

Before you were confirmed, of course you already have drawn from your own experiences.

For several years you've been going through the transition process.

I'm thinking of the time when granny and I met you by chance at "Paleet" the first time you went down into town on an excursion with you class.

We all experience an infinities of new experiences and that applies for as long as you live.

For some, the transition from childhood to adulthood lasts a long time, while for others it goes more quickly.

You have been lucky, incredibly lucky with your "judges". Here I would like to add, however, that they have had several "assistant judges", not least your godfather, Jon, whom I know has been of great support to you.

You have grown up with a mum and dad who have a wide experience of life and its challenges, but they've also have had their share of hardships.

One day you will also understand and acknowledge that it is through challenges and hardship that one learns and grows, not so much when one is surfing downwind.

You have acquired a lot with ease, but you have also met some challenges. So far it seems as though you're handling these in a good way but here, as in all other situations in life, it's all about not giving up.

There are no limits to what you can do, Oscar, but it's important that you focus on what you wish to achieve. Try to put yourself into a situation where you have already accomplished what you wish to achieve. Get in touch with and taste how it feels and ask yourself if the result is the way you imagined it would be.

If you're not happy with it, there's no shame in turning back or trying a different direction.

However, it so happens that it isn't always right to fight tooth and nail in order to make the transition from childhood to adulthood as short as possible, it should just be as right as possible.

Only then, when the transition is right, will you feel sufficiently secure to make important future decisions, both for yourself and others.

There's an expression which says that good advice is expensive. I'm not so sure that that's always correct. If you're attentive and alert, you can get a lot for free.

No one can give you a recipe for a happy life and no one can say that if you do things in such and such a way, everything will end well. Of course, it can be said, but there is no guaranteed result?

It is, once again, up to you.

Be curious about life, be curious about everything, ask questions, be active and don't let the world pass by without getting involved.
Seize the opportunities when they appear.
Use but don't abuse.
Be open, remember nothing enters into a closed hand.
A rule which never fails is that pride comes before a fall.
Smile even though it isn't always easy.
Be polite and attentive and don't forget the importance of being a good listener.
Learn languages and use them to get insight into other cultures.
Behave towards others as you expect them to behave towards you.

Be aware of your responsibilities but, at the same time, don't forget that you also have your own life to live.

With this advice as part of your rules in life, as well as a reasonable obedience to the ten commandments, which you have probably brushed up on during the preparation for your confirmation, you ought to be well-equipped to meet the world which lies at your feet.

Granny and I love you very much and I'm proud to be your "Bappi".

A toast from all of us to wish you all the best, Oscar.

Oslo 4.8.2011

The middle way

The answer is always the middle way
so it was with Aristotle and so it is today.
GM

Prestige

April 2013

This is concerned with reputation, which makes it both quite personal and difficult. Unfortunately that which is personal can easily become uncomfortable. It is a protected world, where others have no right to be, or have they?

For some, prestige has no meaning in their daily lives, whereas for others it is vital and counts every hour of the day, all year round. It is this prestige I'd like to dwell on a bit. I've experienced various sides of it but have to admit that my experiences haven't always been positive. Not that they have been important to me, but I have found people concerned with prestige to be navigating in their own world. If they themselves are aware of this it has to be their own decision, but perhaps prestige acts as a protective shell, something one can hide behind in order not to be too transparent? Perhaps its prestige which makes them function and gives them purpose in their everyday life?

The most important aspect is not what they themselves represent but what they believe they represent to those around them. The strange thing is that if they don't come across as people who share their values, then they pull out their entire arsenal, as it becomes really important for them to leave a prestige-filled impression. Is it done to impress or, once again, is it to hide something?

There is often no limit to what others offer by way of conversation and certain pet topics are frequently repeated. I've thought about whether there is something deeper behind this. Is it the case that people who seem to have experienced most things in life feel that it's still important to give the impression that they have done even more than they really have? Is it a built-in inadequacy or perhaps an additional need to hide something, which has to be satisfied?

Up to now it has all been about verbal prestige, but that's only one of its facets. Expressions like, "that lends prestige to the person in question" or, "that's a prestigious position" speak for themselves and carry no judgements.

Used in such contexts, there are no negative thoughts behind them.

What about the type of prestige which has to do with trends and status?

Trends are normally something which concerns the younger generation and though they are seldom so far along in life, that prestige - the way I see it - has taken root in their consciousness.

Young people just want whatever it is because others have it and because it's trendy. This is rightly called peer pressure.

I've got a bit of a problem seeing the difference between prestige and status, but I am sure there is a difference. The struggle for social status for instance has more to do with living up to other people's standards,and the wish not to be different.

Status symbol is the name given to that which one outwardly acquires in the form of prestigious cars, boats, etc. This type of prestige goes deep with a lot of people.

I remember well, when my then common-law wife, who a year later became my lawfully wedded wife, got her first Hyundai Coupé in 1997. She bought it on my recommendation. I had been around to Oslo's car dealerships with my son-in-law to have a look at their selection. I don't remember the name of the dealership, but we noticed a car I thought looked very stylish in the car park outside. It turned out to be a Hyundai Coupé which belonged to the sales manager and was the only one at the time of its kind to have been imported. I talked to my wife on the phone that same afternoon and she started her local enquiries immediately. By chance she heard that a car dealership in the town, Cuevas de Almanzora, half an hour's drive from where we lived, had become a Hyundai agent. She ordered the car unseen and had it delivered after a fortnight.

My surprise was great when she met me at the airport with her newly acquired car after my visit to Norway. She hadn't mentioned anything to me about the purchase.

My wife has since had two further cars of the Coupé type and changed just a few months ago to a smaller model, the i30. I have had two Hyundai Santa Fes. The last one I had for seven years and we can't express how happy we are and have been with all of them. I'm not being paid by Hyundai for these superlatives, even though it might seem so. I won't mention what brand of car I'm currently driving as it might upset my idea of prestige.

So where does prestige enter into it? Well, it took several years before one could talk openly about the Hyundai brand in Norway. One also didn't see many of them on the roads and there definitely wasn't any prestige or status involved in driving this brand, in fact, it was rather embarrassing. Prestige and status meant driving Audi, Mercedes and BMW, only then did one belong.

Eventually more Santa Fes were being used as taxis and today one probably talks about both KIA and Hyundai as drivable vehicles, but there's no prestige in driving either of them, as I understand - at least not in Norway.

No, the similarity or difference between prestige and status, I can't seem to come to grips with, so I'll try to stick with pure prestige.

I can't help mentioning an example which must have gone quite deep. A friend of mine, an employer, once told me of a work problem.

In a difficult economic period lay-offs became necessary. A particular person held a high position, had for years performed impeccably for the firm, but finally the day of his redundancy had arrived. The person, who understood the reason behind the lay-offs, offered to take a drastic drop in salary or to change his position internally, but he insisted his title must be kept.

I'm inclined to draw the conclusion that it must have been his social status as well as prestige which caused this reaction.

Here we go again, prestige and status.

Something more down to earth, in 2002 the biggest oil spill in the history of Spain, Portugal and France took place. Hundreds if not thousands of kilometres of beaches were destroyed when an enormous tanker broke in half and went down on the Spanish north-west coast. The name of the tanker was "Prestige" and it spilled 630,000 tons of oil.

Prestige in my opinion doesn't guarantee anything at all.

What a good life we could live if we could avoid stupidity.
GM

San Roque

Feb. 2014

That time goes quickly we all know and that the speed with which it passes becomes even greater with age, is clear to those of us who have been allowed to live this long.

One's memory gradually worsens too, but the good thing is that one occasionally catches glimpses of past experiences and when one does, and they are of a character one would like to share with others, they can become quite clear both as pictures and events.

Various reference books are also a great help, when one wants to refresh certain details when necessary.

San Roque is a well-known golfing location in the South of Spain, near Gibraltar, and it's a simple episode from there that I would like to share with others.

The legend, Seve Ballesteros, is known to golfers world-wide for his merits from the mid-seventies to the mid-nineties.

Born in the North of Spain on the 9th of April, 1957, the year in which I got my driving licence while at school in Italy, he grew up in a so-called golfing family where everyone, in some form or other, was involved with golf.

During his active career he won, among others, 90 international tournaments. His so-called Natural Golf School is located at the San Roque Club and is run by his brother Vicente, who worked as his caddy for many years.

Ballesteros died on the 7th of May, 2011, only 54 years old.

In connection with one of our many trips to Gibraltar, during the second half of the nineties, my wife and I had booked a couple of nights at San Roque.

The idea was to play golf and spend a couple of pleasant days there.

After having arrived and been shown to the little bungalow we had booked, it must have been early in the year, we discovered that it hadn't been cleaned nor made ready and was freezing cold. My better half doesn't accept such states of affair without taking action, so it wasn't long before alternative accommodation had been provided. To this part of the story has to be added that after our visit she wrote, in perfect Spanish, of course, a letter to the management, which was answered immediately with an infinite number of extenuating excuses. San Roque is after all a five star establishment.

I seem to recall that the Japanese had bought the place at this point and that a first-class Sushi bar and restaurant was visited with great pleasure on our first evening.

The next morning we had booked tee-off time at "The Old Course". This course, which is 6,494 meters and 72 par, was originally designed by Dave Thomas in 1990, while the bunkers were updated by Ballesteros at a later date. How one can be certain that it is exactly 6,494 meters, no more and no less, and how the measurements were done, I don't know, of course, but as with everything else within golf, there are probably detailed rules for this too.

The day dawns to bright sunshine and we present ourselves to the starter at the first hole with time to spare. With all documents in order and both sets of clubs in the golf buggy we're ready to go. No one else has shown up, so there's just the two of us teeing off. We can't see anyone ahead of us either, so this looks to be a peaceful round without any stress whatsoever.

The signs clearly state that one must only drive on the designated paths along the course and not on the course itself.

My wife normally finds it a waste of energy to warm up before a round of golf, so when we play together, I also forego my normal obligatory bucket of balls at the driving range.

She normally plays equally well without a warm-up, whereas for me a lack of warm-up generally results in bad scores at the first holes.

As usual, there were several bunker shots at holes 1 and 2. Hole 3, the 143 meter par 3 hole, with a small green much lower than the tee, however, went well. We had an impressive view towards the urbanization on the other side of the valley.

We are ready for the fourth. No other players in sight, 330 meters to the flag from the yellow tee place for men and 285 for women's red. My drive ends among the pines to the left of the fairway and a bit higher up, whereas my wife's is perfectly placed on the right. Since the path is on the right, she takes the buggy while I, equipped with several clubs, continue on shank's pony towards the left.

What we hadn't seen while teeing off was that a ridge to the right of the fairway hid a slightly lower point in front of the bunker. On the way towards my ball I see my wife stop at her ball, which lies a good distance from the ridge, getting ready to strike. At the same moment, I see two people between her and the green, something she naturally enough can't see. I immediately register that it is Seve Ballesteros standing there, with a photographer at the ready, and a wedge in his hand.

I have from the very first day of our relationship, called my wife by her first name, Euphrosine, or, to make it easier for others to understand me, my little wife, as Euphrosine for most people hasn't got any meaning at all and would thus only rarely be considered a name. Furthermore, I had at that time not quite mastered the correct pronunciation of Euphrosine, which meant that I managed to stop her shot by shouting: "Look out my little wife, there are people in front of you".

After my loud apology for having shouted, Seve bursts out laughing and says:
"It's the first time I've heard someone shout something like that on a golf course".

Immediately afterwards he smilingly apologized for being where they were on the course, and waved my wife through. After this little episode, naturally neither of us managed par at hole 4.

Back at the clubhouse there are nods of recognition when he passes our table on the way to his three children and his then wife, Carmen.

Another broad smile followed by: "My little wife" and a slight shake of his head.

Will

From this ridge my belief can build a bridge
just put me to the test, I'll do all the rest.
He's mad as a hatter – it's all nonsense his natter -
is he totally bent, has he lost his scent?
GM

Secret

April 2013

Everyone has experience when it comes to secrets, both good or bad.

Whether it is a secret all one's own or a secret shared with others, it's on our mind. One is always reminded of it, as one mustn't in any way reveal it to anyone, as then it would no longer be a secret.

Is there something called a public secret? The expression is often heard when it has to do with something the public knows without its having been publicly confirmed. I believe the expression to be apt.

Another public secret, but seen from a slightly different angle, is the book titled, "The Secret". It is written by Rhonda Byrne. It is, of course, the opposite of a public secret, it isn't a secret at all, as it can be bought and read by everyone.

My wife and I were given it as a present from a very pleasant professional woman golfer, with whom we played together in a so-called pro-am, professional amateur competition, at our local golf course, Valle del Este, where we are members. Her name is Alison, she's from England and her greeting written in the book says: "To George and Marianne, I hope this book brings you as much joy, inspiration and happiness as it has to me. Lots of love, Alison".

I have read the book several times with great pleasure and recommend it to all those who are curious about life and open to unusual ideas.

I have given it to several friends in different languages.

We also have what is called a white lie, the innocent one; the one which smooth's things over and doesn't start the boat rocking.

Does the same thing exist as regards secrets, is there a white one? An innocent secret, one which is based on one's feeling a bit guilty at having held something back, but something which one considers relatively trifling in its context. A trifling secret? It has to be of so little importance that it doesn't really matter if it doesn't remain a secret, so why not just get rid of it?

It strikes me that one of the really big secrets remained a secret even though it has to have been known by a large number of people.

It is said that the last world war was shortened considerably just because those involved managed to keep the secret without it becoming known by the Germans. I'm here thinking of the well-known German built encryption machines called "Enigma". These had been developed gradually from the end of the First World War and were used by the German military in almost all types of communication towards and during all of the last great war.

In May 1941 the German submarine U-110 was hijacked by the British, complete with Enigma machine, codebook and manual. All told, the allies reportedly managed to lay their hands on 7 or 8 of these machines with accessories.

Top people from several countries were set to work on breaking the codes, something they ultimately managed not least with the aid of specialists from Poland and Alan Turing.

From then on one could, with a large degree of accuracy, keep track of the communication within the different German weapons branches and, not least, between the bases and the submarines.

Then one can ask oneself how it was possible that this wasn't known to the Germans, even though they probably suspected that the allies in some way or other had access to the information? Investigation committees were formed, not least because of Karl Dönitz suspicions that the allied had broken the Enigma code, but it was never proven.

The incredible thing about this secret, which after all was known by many people, was that it was never passed on to the Germans.

What then about Operation Overlord and the allied invasion of Normandy on D-day the 6th of June 1944?

Here there must have been countless people involved. Even a month after the Normandy landings, the Germans seemed to believe that this was a diversion and that the actual landing would take place in the Calais region.

No one can say for sure what the keeping of this secret meant to the duration of the war, but one thing is certain, that if the Germans had had all their resources together at the right place, much would have been different.

Again, how is it possible for the Normandy landings to have remained a secret?

In all fairness, the British had created clever diversions in the form of artificial aeroplanes, tanks and other equipment made of canvas and plywood, which they placed in the South East of England, in other words near the shortest crossing between France and England, where the Germans thought the invasion would take place. Their observations from the air clearly indicated that this was where preparations were being made.

These two last examples of secrets are probably relatively unususl, even though it is important also in peacetime for nations to protect their interests and they thus often resort to secrecy.

Why would one need spies if this weren't the case?

As far as more down to earth and innocent secrets go, it is probably the female part of the population which takes the lead.

Here it ranges from "secret uplifts" to hidden inlays of various types both here and there, as well as major and minor surgery to make corrections which one believes will lead to greater beauty.

Most of these secrets are in reality never really secret. Men are probably not as naïve as women would like to believe, but who wants to tear down someone's self-esteem if a few secrets would otherwise make the person happy. So Ladies, keep your secrets, men also need their stimulus.

There are various statistics to do with the amount of time women spend on themselves in connection with their looks. No secret there. Nor when it comes to women's most hated time consumption to do with themselves. I saw it published in a paper a few days ago, so that at least is no secret.

59 days of her life a woman spends on the most hated of self-care, the shaving of her legs. The research shows that 35% of all women find this activity a chore and thus hate it the most. Most of them spend four minutes a day removing hair from their legs, six days a week, or a total of 21 hours a year.

Number two on the list is hair-care. 17% feel it's a chore having to do it, but admit to spending 16 minutes a day throughout their lives doing it, which means a total of 294 days. Number three on the list of the most hated self-care, is the plucking of eyebrows. 14% mean that this is also a chore, which totals 11 hours a year.

If someone feels this should be kept secret, it is, as one can see, too late.

The greatest and most significant secrets are in my opinion those of nature. More and more are being revealed, but it is with this as with the drop in the ocean, there has to be an infinite number of them, which is only to the good.

The world will never run out of secrets.

Thank you

Dear God look after my thoughts in the now -
as it is you who decide where they go.
Regardless where I want them to lead me to -
let my subconscious decide, what <u>you</u> want me to do.
A thought is tax-free and has no borders -
for us that is but you give the orders.
You know what we're thinking, when our defences are sink-
ing -
as you open and close the chains that are linking.
GM

Stories from Landøya

May 2013

I came to Landøya in Asker for the first time at the end of the summer in 1946. Max, my stepfather, had bought the property on Landøya, called Norderhaug, from the Directorate for Compensation. It was lightly smaller than 20 acres. I won't here go into what the Directorate stood for, but for those of you who might be interested, all you have to do is look it up. I was 7 years old at the time and came directly from Sweden.

What I want to do with these stories is to present some of my memories from those days, without putting them in any chronological order or priority; they'll just appear as they do in my memory.

I have to emphasize once again that some of these stories goes almost seventy years in time, so no one should take too much notice of the dates or expect detailed accuracy in what they are reading. I would like those who might wish to, to get a general impression of how I remember episodes from that time through today's eyes and with a memory which is bound to be biased.

The setting should probably be explained more closely before I begin.

If one can imagine a former farm with a relatively modest-looking main house, the earliest foundations of which are almost 200 years old, a middle house and a barn, all painted red, strategically placed on a property comprised of a reasonably large apple orchard, a duck pond and surrounded by a wood consisting of birch, pine and spruce trees, then the picture should be complete.

To the north, the property is open towards a fairly steep cliff and a wide valley.

Today Landøya is a peninsula but in ancient times, some 1500 years ago it is said, it was an island, thus its name, I believe.

A middle house between the main house and a barn, as well as a hen house fifty meters from the barn were also part of the property, both painted the same colour as the rest.

The Rolls of Film

The reason I call this story the rolls of film, is because the box I had found in the cellar contained several rolls of film as well as a number of notebooks, photographs and documents.

I believe this took place shortly after we moved there. In other words, I had just turned seven and can't remember what caused me to move the box from the cellar and into the garden but, as we will see, it was probably a good thing that I did.

Nor can I explain how I knew that film burnt in a special sizzling way, as if it were fireworks, or if I knew anything about it at all.

The remaining contents of the box I can't have had any understanding of or interest in and I can't remember if I had removed any of it from the box. Anyway the child pyromaniac went to work.

I expect I had removed at least one of the films from its spool before lighting the match. This had barely reached the end of the film before the fireworks got started. It wouldn't be right for me to go into details about the event, as it would be pure fiction. The long and short of it is that the box contained films Max had taken during the war and most of the illegal and legal documentation he had used as a saboteur.

I believe Max regarded me in a special way after this, something which I can fully understand. He wasn't used to children, since he had never had any. Then he got presented with this problem by a new child who had just been part of the family when he dad moved into a new relationship with his mother.

Anyway, I don't think everything went up in flames, but I understand very well that it must have been terrible for him to lose even a part of what was in the box, no doubt it was all of invaluable historical content.

The Duck Pond

At the bottom of the apple orchard in front of the main house and the middle house and bordering our neighbour's property, was what I remember as the duck pond. Called that, of course, because it in the summer season was inhabited by ducks. The pond, which is still there, isn't especially big, perhaps fifteen to twenty meters across. It wasn't fenced in when we moved there, but a family film from the incredibly warm and beautiful summer of 1947, shows that it had been sur-rounded by a white picket fence on all sides except towards the neighbour where there already was a mesh fence.

Our neighbour's house was well away, so the pond lay undisturbed, close to our driveway. I think the fence was put up so that my half-brother, Lillemax, who was born that year, wouldn't get into trouble and, of course so that the English Setter Pet, was unable to get at the ducks, which in the season seemed to thrive in their little paradise.

I seem to remember that there even was a little red painted duck house in the pond, trimmed in white just like all the other houses.

At the right time of year, there was, of course, a deafening noise from the frogs which must also have thrived there together with the ducks. The ducks must, however, have been hard of hearing to be able to co-exist with them, but that's a different matter.

For a period of time after the war, Max had placed a rubber dingy there, which I believe he had used during the attacks on Oslo harbour in the war.

In the wintertime our gang of boys got out the spades and made sure the pond was always free of snow and ready for skating. Ice hockey was popular but I can't remember our having anything but screw-on skates in this early period after the war and we had to make the sticks ourselves.

As the years went by, we outgrew the pond and it was the boys' ice-hockey team at Holmen which kept us occupied, while Lillemax later took over our old arena with slightly more graceful movements.

The most exciting activity when it came to the pond was to see how long after the melting of the snow, the ice would hold before we went through.

One of us always came out the winner before the season changed and we went on to other activities.

The Lawnmower

A hedge consisting of black and red currant bushes forms a barrier between the apple orchard, which is situated by the duck pond, and the driveway. It stretches from the gate, past the garage and the middle house, all the way to the main house. On the corner outside the garage, there's a gap in the hedge allowing direct access to the apple orchard without having to walk all the way around.

The gap in the hedge is the reason why this story was put to paper.

The entire apple orchard was sown with grass, except directly below the apple trees where there were circles of earth with a diameter of a few meters.

I wouldn't call it lawn according to today's norms but regardless, it was regularly cut. A terrible job when it had to be done with a normal manual lawnmower.

How Max managed to acquire a brand new motorized lawnmower so early after the war, I have no idea, but the marvel had at least arrived. No one had ever seen such a machine in our area, so all the boys in the gang had gathered to watch its trial run. At a respectful distance we stared as Max manoeuvred it down through the orchard leaving behind a close-cropped path about one meter wide.

After the demonstration it remained standing down by the pond, awaiting its restart later on for an attack on the entire apple orchard.

It was late afternoon before the mower was started up again and the cutting began. I followed behind Max and watched his every manoeuvre, certain that I would quite soon be able to do the cutting myself.

The entire apple orchard had to be cut and it was already getting dark when the machine, having completed its task, had to be taken through the gap in the current hedge and into the garage. Just there there was some uneven and loose earth, causing the wheels to slip and the machine to come to a stop, even though the motor continued to run. Max made several attempts at moving ahead but without success.

What was then more natural than that I should try to help, and my right hand shot out toward the lateral brace in front of the rotating cutting blades themselves, which I because of the dark couldn't see and thus didn't know were still rotating. With a loud scream I snatched my hand back again and registered that blood was spurting from both my index and middle fingers. Max quickly turns off the motor whereupon I was given a resounding slap across my ear. Only then did he become aware of what had happened.

Full speed to the nearest doctor, who found that the fingers with some luck might be saved, but that it was a question of no more than a millimetre.

After an injection, a few stitches and a big bandage, we went back home.

It took a bit more time than I had expected before I was allowed to do the motorized grass cutting on my own.

I've never again been able to bend my right hand index finger the same way as my left, but it has never prevented me from hunting and shooting clay pigeons, my two great hobbies before golf took over later in life.

The Executioner's Assistant

I believe I mentioned in the introduction that there was also a hen house on the property. This was situated only a stone's throw from the barn, where the "Tower House" is located today, partly shaded by large pines. It was also painted red with white gables like the other houses on the property.

Apart from a fenced in area of about fifty square meters, which constituted the hen house yard itself, this was also where the vegetable garden was found. Here everything from lettuce and radishes to carrots and dill was grown.

I even had my own little section which I proudly looked after. Even in those days I believe it became clear that I had so-called green thumbs though it didn't influence my later life.

The hen yard was so constructed that the hens could freely go into and out of it from the hen house. This was designed in such a way that each hen had its own little cubicle and I seem to recall that there were around twenty hens there at any one time.

Since I, at the time, was only seven or eight years old, I wasn't especially interested in how they multiplied, but a regal rooster was always with them and there was no lack of new generations. How the practical aspect of it was handled I don't remember, but that new arrivals were needed was obviously due to there also being departures.

How often some of them were put to death, I don't remember, but the ritual was the same in summer as in winter.

The only heating to be found in the houses on the property came from Jøtul stoves and fireplaces, so we needed the woodshed, which was an extension to the left of the barn, in other words, a stone's throw from the hen house. From there, it was my job to collect the axe, while the executioner, Max, straightened the special chopping block, which was placed in front of the hen house, to make sure it was standing firm. It was, after all, used in all seasons, and as it was a matter of precision, everything had to be in order.

Those of the hens which were inside during this execution had, as one might understand from this, the best view.

If the choice was made according to age, weight or egg production shall remain unsaid, but for the unlucky one or ones, it was I who led the goodbyes.

With one hand on each side of the hen and with its head facing forward, I headed towards the executioner. I can assure the readers that a hen has immense strength and I assume especially so when it feels that its last minutes are approaching, thus it happened on occasion that it got free of my embrace and went flapping away. Then, after a powerful telling off from the executioner, I had to run after it and try to catch it again.

Anyway, it understandably ended up with its neck and head on the chopping block and the executioner's precision led to a painless transition into its eternal pecking paradise. I expect that's the way it should works, but it didn't look like it at first. I've never seen any hens run faster than the ones without heads.

The flapping run never lasted long, however, but I do know that new local speed records for headless hens running in zigzag or circles were often set in front of the red hen house, a stone's throw from the barn.

One can, of course, ask oneself if it would be natural in Norway nowadays to let a seven or eight year old child be the executioner's assistant, but so many things were very different in those days.

My Swiss wife, when I told her this story, recognized the technique from her own grandmother's farm in Gros de Vaud, when she visited there as a child, the only difference being that the method obviously was a bit more sophisticated and less labour intensive than the one we used at Landøya.

The grandmother herself put the hens under her left arm and did the work with the axe in her right hand, in other words, without an assistant.

Bog Hill

Between the main house and the traditional outhouse, there is a hill which runs from the barn at the top all the way to the bottom of the apple orchard. The difference in height must be between fifteen and twenty meters and thus was more than enough to construct ski jumps of various kinds, according to the requirements of the boys in the gang.

It started out with an apple crate as the jump itself and we achieved lengths of about two or three meters, which the family still has films of, and moved gradually upwards until we advanced and built the so-called, Bog Hill. It was given its name because it was situated only ten or fifteen meters from the outhouse and because the place itself was well suited for a ski jump, the hill having a natural knoll and landing slope. We were mainly into ski jumping, as the other winter sports such as cross country skiing and slalom were virtually unknown in our area in those days.

Much of our inspiration came from the fact that a well-known ski jumper called Georg Thrane was our next door neighbour. The brothers, Asbjørn and Sigmund Ruud were ski jumping stars already known worldwide and with Olympic Medals, but they lived in Kongsberg, many hours from us by car, whereas Georg Thrane was our closest neighbour and represented Asker Ski Club, the most well-known club in our area. One can imagine the sort of model he was, especially after he won the internationally known Holmenkollen Ski Jumping Event in 1947.

Furthermore, he was the first to introduce what was naturally called the "Thrane Style".

The majority jumped with a so-called "hip bend" and with their arms stretched out in front or to the sides as though they were wings. Thrane on the other hand, put his arms along his sides toward the back, the way one sees today's jumpers do, as they soar aerodynamically through the air.

For us, the Thrane Style was the only one worthwhile.

When Bog Hill was finally finished, it looked really elegant through our eyes. The take-off ramp started up by the barn and went down the hill without the need of any artificial aid. On the other hand, the transition from the ramp to the jump as well as the, more than one meter high, jump itself were the object of several days of work every year.

If I say that we were able to jump about ten meters, I'm not exaggerating.

No one had jumping skis, but used whatever they had. The most important thing was to have bindings which didn't allow too much distance from the heels of the boots to the skis. Otherwise the skis would be blown straight up and one would invariably land on one's back on the landing slope.

If one were lucky enough to end upright, everything went well for the first fifteen meters after landing, but then one had to react quickly, dodging to the right and left to avoid colliding with the apple trees.

This done, it was essential to make an abrupt stop as quickly as possible, before ending up in the mesh fence at the cliff, which formed the north side of the property.

There was a ski jumping competition every year with prizes of different kinds and with participants from the entire area. There was no lack of determination.

For my part, it became worse as I later got proper jumping skis. Then it all became more serious.

It went well at first. I participated in a series of ski jumping events and at times there were even prizes to be had.

All this took place at the ski jumps for boys with jumps of fifteen or twenty meters. The style was never lacking, but having the courage to put enough effort into the length was a different matter, as it was proportional to the size of the hill.

I seem to remember that my jumping career culminated on the big Holmen Hill, not to be confused with Holmenkollen Hill, when I once, after having put a lot of effort into overcoming my fear, finally set off.

The Thrane Style had worked reasonably well on the hills for boys, but here, where one jumped fifty to sixty meters, things were different. Down the ramp I went with my arms along my sides in excellent Thrane Style, until I came up over the knoll and could see what lay in front of me. Suddenly my arms went out to the sides but without my bending at the hip. The tips of the skis were pushed straight up in the air and then I went down, arms flapping. The jump, if one can call it a jump, ended with me on my back down on the landing slope. The style was probably OK the first second after leaving the edge of the jump, but then fear took over.

It was the person jumping who failed.

The length only counts if you finish standing, so I can't say that I jumped about forty meters. Even though I wasn't hurt in any way, it remained my only attempt.

I was far better suited to cross country skiing in the latter part of my adolescence.

Grandfather

Grandfather, Max's father, was born in 1877 and was probably the person I looked up to the most during the post-war years - he was around seventy at the time. I remember him especially at Christmas when he came to visit us from Lærdal where he lived; I believe that for me some valuable ties of friendship were made.

He was in my memory a peaceful man, who seldom got angry, with a charisma and humanity which was always touched with warmth and peace.

Not only did he normally look like Father Christmas, but with an artificial beard - he had an imposing moustache himself - he played the role of Father Christmas on Christmas Eve. From the main house we could, in the light from the lamps on the gateposts, see him coming, dragging a large sack behind him.

If I could ever be like him with my grandchildren, I would be greatly privileged.

He took the name Juan Manus, converted from Johan Magnussen. This more Latin sounding name, he adopted after having lived for a number of years in Spanish speaking countries.

I especially remember our walks to Petter Dalen; I believe it must have been an ironmonger's shop, a few kilometres from Landøya. It was the nearest place to buy Christmas presents; the first time we were there I was allow to choose which sheath knife I wanted.

I'll never forget the safe feel of the hand I was holding, when grandfather and I toddled off along the road past Holmen country store and on to Ravnsborg, where the shop was situated.

His summer visits I also remember as being very special. It was said about grandfather, and probably rightly so, that he lived like a hermit up there in Lærdal. His life was mostly about hunting and fishing.

Unfortunately I was never to visit him there, but Max joined him on several occasions to hunt.

He lived in a little house in Lærdal itself but also had a little cabin in the mountains where he stayed during the hunting season. How he ended up where he lived, I don't know, but I've heard several stories at various occasions throughout the years from people who knew about him.

He was probably seen as somewhat special, but he was liked by everyone. He was, among other things, a translator in several languages and had been married to a Danish woman, Gerda Kiørup, Max's mother.

With her I later established closer contact through our Danish firm, which was started by Max in 1957.

Life in Copenhagen probably became too cramped for my grandfather, with his inborn hunting and fishing interests, and sometime in the thirties they got divorced. He took Max and his youngest sister Pia with him and moved to Oslo, while their mother and two other sisters, Bente and Carmen remained in Copenhagen.

Back to grandfather; by far the most important person in this little story. He was a passionate pipe smoker and was seldom without his curved pipe in his mouth.

We had been to Petter Dalen and bought what we needed to make a crow trap.

After having brought this home we gathered together the necessary tools, some wire cutters, a hammer, a saw, and, of course, the sheath knife - I had already been given mine and he always carried his on his belt, we were ready.

All this equipment was then carried into the woods behind the football field. There we settled down and operation crow trap got under way.

First grandfather explained everything about the intelligence of the crows, their reaction, their justifiable and non-justifiable role in nature and a great number of examples of this, which made me stare at him wide-eyed.

I no longer remember the details, of course, but that they made an impression on me there is no doubt about; my vivid imagination got nicely fertilized.

The making of the trap itself was after this seen in a special light. Crows, because at the time there were probably too many, could be shot and when the feet were delivered to the police, there was a reward. I seem to remember that it was two kroner a pair at the time, but I can't vouch for it.

The trap we made wasn't to be used to trap the crows and then kill them, as that was cowardly, it was the thrill of the catch itself which was important, and they would, if they got into the trap, be set free again.

To the wooden board which formed the base, thick steel wire braces were fastened and these were in turn covered with chicken wire, which was fastened with a thinner steel wire. One of the end walls was covered with chicken wire which was fastened with a thinner steel wire. One of the end walls was covered with chicken wire whereas the other was equipped with a simple steel-wire-framed door, which could only be opened inward. So far it had been relatively simple and most of the day had gone.

The whole time grandfather was working on the trap, he was telling me stories from nature, all this as he let me perform minor tasks such as cutting suitable lengths of steel wire to fasten the chicken wire with.

Even though we were only a few hundred meters from the main house, he had brought a packed lunch and something to drink, so that became a real excursion into nature.

The next day time came to create the more intricate tilting device inside the trap, the one which, when the crow stepped onto it, would cause the door to drop down behind it. The door was basically fastened to the roof of the trap and was released by its connection to the tilting device. "Voìla", the crow was caught, that is if it had been tempted by the bait placed at the far edge of the tilting device.

120

I don't remember what grandfather used as bait but believe it was mice we had caught in the cellar of the main house.

Crows were caught and set free, but as with everything else, when the novelty had worn off and grandfather disappeared back to Lærdal, the eagerness to catch crows also disappeared.

Even today, almost seventy years later, the memory of my grandfather and his crow cage stands out as one of my best memories.

The Linoleum Floor

Had it only been what we associate with a normal linoleum floor, this story would never have seen any print.

Linoleum is a material used among other things as floor covering. This consists of linoleum, resin and cork, to which dye has been added and then placed on rough burlap. When the joints have been properly sealed, the covering is also water-tight.

As soon as it has been laid, it can be used.

There was a shortage of all types of materials after the war, however, and for some reason there was a sort of liquid linoleum which instead of being rolled out and glued to the floor beneath it, was poured onto the floor and spread out evenly across the entire floor surface.

This type had to be left to dry for some time before it could be used.

It was only later that this became clear to me.

As a nature lover, one of the first installations Max built in the main house was a sauna. This was put in the cellar after a proper cement floor had been laid.

The framework and insulated walls were already in place, the door had been put in and the wood stove would be installed when the floor had been laid.

Next to the sauna a shower had been installed in a separate room, complete with a proper drain and ventilation.

No sauna without a shower.

I had strict orders not to disturb the workers laying the floor and took this seriously.

As usually there was a group of boys playing football on the field in front of the house. This happened more or less every day, as it formed a natural part of one's free time.

When today various soccer players perform in all kinds of coloured football boots, in those days there was no access to such things. What sort of boots professional football players wore in those days, I don't know, but the nearest we mortals came to such things, was to buy so-called knobs. These were made of several layers of thick leather, were circle-shaped and I believe approximately 2 centimetres high. Three solid nails kept them together in addition to them having been glued, and a bit more than one centimetre of the nails stuck out so that they could be fastened to the sole of a boot.

This had to be done by a shoemaker as he had a so-called "iron foot" which he placed inside the boot before he hammered in the nails. When the three nails hit the iron foot they bent, which made it impossible to remove the knob before it was worn out. As for boots, they were in short supply, thus well-worn welt boots were used. Not everyone was fortunate enough to have access to this equipment, but the lucky ones obviously achieved a higher status than those without. I, who had lived for a while during the war in Ulvik in Hardanger, with my mother's sister, auntie Kari, and my elder cousins, had inherited boots from them, so I was among the privileged ones.

The sun had already set behind the horizon and the workers had long since left the scene, having finished the work on the floor covering.

I was, of course, more than a little proud of the new sauna, none of us boys in the gang had seen anything like it, and so what was more natural than that I should offer them a tour.

It was, however, quite dark in the cellar as the electrical installation wasn't finished, but a quick look should be possible.

I open the door and am the first to enter the mystical "sweat room". Knobs at the bottom of the shoes or not, the floor would probably have been ruined anyway. It was too late to be sorry, it couldn't be undone. The linoleum mixture already had dozens of knob imprints which could not be erased.

Due to the bad light we couldn't see the full extent of the damage, but understood that it was serious.

To make a long story short, if it qualified for four or five strokes from the dog whip, I can't remember, but there's no doubt about it hurting a lot.

However, the punishment hasn't stopped me from becoming an avid sauna user over the years.

122

The Gondola Lift

My using this title must be seen in the context of an eight or ten year old having a somewhat different perspective than he does later on at a more mature age.

First a short explanation as regards the barn. It consisted of two floors, with a staircase in the middle of an open-fronted covered recess, which formed a roughly fifty square meter stone-paved sort of terrace. Note that I write "consisted of". Later, in a different story, one will understand why.

On both sides, from the middle sloping roof on the second floor, there was a seemingly large room which could be used by summer guests staying over-night. On the left, on the first floor, seen from the front, from the location of the hen house, there was an apartment with a kitchen, sitting-room and bedroom and on the right, a room the same size as the one above.

In the apartment lived an elderly couple, Mr. and Mrs. Bergstrøm, for free, as he did various odd-jobs around the place.

Among other things, he was responsible for chopping wood. All our heating in winter came from wood stoves, in the main house, the middle house and the barn. For this purpose a roof had been constructed over a space on the left side of the barn, again seen from the front, below the window in the room above.

Here a lorry load of wood was delivered every year, which had to be cut, split and stacked, in readiness for the winter.

The large open room on the second floor, between the two end rooms, was in winter a favoured place to play, especially since all manner of things, which couldn't be stored elsewhere, were placed there. There were often confrontations with the Bergstrøms when the noise level from the boys in the gang, especially on rainy days, put their family peace to the test.

This story would not have been written if the wood stoves in the Bergstrøms' apartment hadn't existed, both the one in the kitchen and the one in the sitting-room, the outlet of which was situated in a brick chimney close to two meter above the barn roof, near the ridge of the roof.

The yard in front of the barn was quite big, almost as big as one's ingenuity.

We had a lot of experience with the so-called lianas growing at different strategic points throughout the property and in the barn there was quite a selection of ropes. I think it must have belonged to the National Guard for whom Max was Area Manager.

A gondola lift hadn't previously entered our minds, but there was a combination of a strong, more than fifty meter long, rope and a chimney on top of a barn as the highest point; we ought to be able to think of something.

Out through the window above the woodpile and from there up onto the ridge of the barn roof was an easy exercise.

One end of the rope was fastened to the upper part of the chimney, the other wound around the bottom of a smallish tree some fifty meters away on the opposite side of the yard in front of the barn. This would provide quite a pleasant gondola trip with a difference in height of about seven or eight meter. An open crate which had earlier been used in connection with the construction of the garage, was perfect for a gondola and with two separate parts of a pulley with drive-wheels fastened to each end of the crate, the contraption was ready to be tested.

Jan, who was a few years older than me and the toughest of us all, signed up as test pilot. He later, in his early twenties, got his licence for small planes. I doubt however that this was inspired by his experience as test pilot of our gondola lift.

Up on the roof they went the test pilot and his helper. To the "gondola" a far thinner rope had been fastened which was now thrown up to the two on the roof. They could then pull the "gondola" up unto the roof and when this was held in place by the helper, Jan got in and sat down. The rest of us stood at the other end of the yard making up the welcoming committee.

The helper lets go and the forward-bending test pilot shoots across the edge of the roof. In about mid-flight it happens; it looks as if one of the pulley wheels has come free. Jan slides with a jerking movement to the front of the "gondola", which suddenly comes to an abrupt; stop about two meters above ground. No one was hurt, but what to do?

Who got to the rope first I don't remember, but eager hands grabbed it, and at a rhythmical pace, in the hope that the "gondola" would start moving again, it was set in motion from side to side.

The impact got greater each time and then it happened. With a terrible crash the "gondola" with its test pilot hit the ground, at the same time as large parts of the chimney in its individual bits and pieces plummeted down from the edge of the roof.

The test pilot got away with nothing but the shock whereas the launching pad, the chimney, was reduced to a height of less than half a meter.

Fortunately the Bergstrøms were not at home and it didn't look like anyone else had noticed what had happened.

It was early in the afternoon, which meant that Max and my mother wouldn't get home from the office until a few hours later.

All hands on deck. At breakneck speed hundreds of bricks were brought up onto the roof, passed out through the window above the wood pile and then on to the ridge of the roof.

Slowly but surely the bricks were placed in such a way as to make it look like the original chimney.

The broken roof tiles represented a bigger challenge. The worst ones were re-placed with others from the roof at the back of the barn, whereas those which were only broken in half, were repositioned as well as could be. The "gondola" was put back where it was found, and the pulley wheels and ropes were put back in their original places.

I can't remember if our escapade was discovered at the time, but I believe I told the story many years later at some occasion, without it having any other conse-quences than a few happy smiles. Both the Bergstrøms and the barn were long gone by then.

The English setter, Pet

One of the first things Max did after moving to Landøya was to acquire an English setter, Pet.

Water had to be fetched from an outdoor well, the electrical installations were at a bare minimum and the main house required much-needed renovation of everything such as for instance a new roof, sanitary equipment and a kitchen.
This was also quite quickly planned and set in motion, while Pet from the very beginning became family member number four.

It was past its puppy stage; I assume Max didn't want to delay his hunting activities more than necessary now that the war was over and his nature instincts could once again seek expression in freedom.

Pet was the black and white type, what I today would characterize as an old-fashioned good-size setter. It immediately became the centre of the family and naturally frolicked freely around the large property and way beyond, as was soon to be seen.

I didn't at the time have any idea of the procreation habits of dogs, but I early on got an insight into why that part of the animal world won't easily disappear.

It sometimes happened that Pet disappeared as if he had no home and stayed away. Then all we could do was wait for the phone to ring. Even on the coldest winter nights with more than twenty degrees below, Pet could lie outside a house where a bitch was on heat. Only when the owners had had enough of the courting dog or if they didn't already know Pet, did they take a look at his collar which showed both name and phone number. Then Max had to go off, sometimes as far as ten kilometres from home, and fetch the spurned lover. I was immediately informed about the cause of his disappearances, so that part of my sex education came at a young age.

Fisher Jørgensen, who lived near the old steamship pier at Landøya, was once given a bad surprise. A so-called "round" birthday was to be celebrated, as we were later given to understand, when the following episode unfolded.

Holmen country store, which was the nearest food store, made deliveries once a week to those of its customers who ordered in advance. Since the store was situated more than a kilometre from home and not many people had cars in those days, this was a good arrangement.

The day of delivery came and we, like several other households on Landøya, were visited by the delivery van. Cardboard boxes were brought into the house and emptied, before they were returned filled with empty bottles of various kinds. The doors of the van were, at least up until this episode, left open, as long as the unloading and loading took place. When the driver returns with the empty bottles, he sees an almost ten meter long snake speeding across the farmyard with Pet in front. We're not really used to snakes in our region and he discovered immediately that it was the sausages meant for Jørgensen's celebratory dinner which were on the run. Shouting and swearing, he went chasing after them as Pet increased his speed with his bounty trailing behind him.

Sausages were a delicacy which couldn't be bought just like that in those days. They had to be ordered far in advance, if one could get them at all, and they weren't delivered one by one separately as today but strung together the way they had been produced.

A great ado resulted, of course, and I don't know how Max finally got out of the bind he was in, but the celebration at the Jørgensens was, if I recall correctly, *despite the incident, carried out with satisfied guests.*

I'll skip what happened to those sausages which hadn't jumped out of their skin, but it shouldn't be too hard to imagine.

As if it were yesterday, I can sense the feeling of safety that came over me after Sunday dinner, as I lay under the grand piano with Pet. The crackling of the fireplace and the voices which could only be heard as incoherent mumbling. The fire noises often lent an extra amount of good feeling to my mother's treatment of the piano keys.

They were among the most peaceful moments of my existence.

"Kiss me once and kiss me twice, then kiss me once again. It's been a long, long time"; one of my mother's favourites. Both the melody and the text have stayed with me since then, as I can't remember ever having heard them since. The meaning of the words I definitely didn't understand.

There's something about animals being intent on defending their territory. One would think that Pet had enough with Norderhaug and its almost twenty acres, but I believe he had greater ambitions. The whole of Landøya suited him better. There's no doubt that this gave him too large a mouthful to digest. Many a time he came ambling home, not exactly with his tail between his legs, but with nasty cuts and gashes, which made clear that his wishes to enlarge his territory hadn't really been profitable. I believe it was especially the English setter belonging to the Stange family which wasn't too happy about the intruder.

Nowadays the "first aid" would probably be performed by a vet, but that type of doctor was unknown in our parts back then.

Max assumed the role of animal doctor with the greatest ease, and had everything at the ready. I especially remember the half-curved needle, which I believe to have been that of a sail-maker. Then the fish tendon, gauze, scissors and, of course, a bottle of iodine. Pet must have early on understood that despite the pain he had to suffer, the treatment was for his own good. He always reconciled himself quickly to the situation. I had the role of holder, comforter and helper, while Max was responsible for the actual "sewing". When the five, ten or fifteen stitches had been done, one had to find methods to avoid the licking of the wound and in this context Max was very inventive.

Even though Pet during his periods of convalescence at times looked somewhat strange, the wounds soon healed, making him ready for further challenges.

Pet was also an eager swimmer and loved the water.

When Max opened the swimming season among the ice floes, often as early as the month of March, Pet was just as eager to be in the water as he was, while we others waited at least two more months before jumping in.

Even from the diving board he jumped, in pure ecstasy, when he saw the rest of us doing it.

I don't remember how old Pet became, but I recall very well that he, with a wooden cross crafted by me, was buried in the north east corner at the bottom of the property.

I have over the years had many four-legged friends of my own, but the first Pet, I'll remember until my dying day.

Reflex

This episode took place on my birthday, the 14th of May. That I remember very well, but don't ask me the exact year. I do believe, however, that I must have been ten or eleven, which means it happened in either 1949 or 50.

The sun was shining as, of course, it should on birthdays when one has behaved well throughout the year. I've grown up with this rule and have always believed in it.

The day must have been a Saturday as both the sausages and the birthday cake had long since been devoured and the football game was going strong, with the sun still high in the sky.

The leaves on the birches had just started to unfold and the flag fluttered lightly in the wind as fifteen to twenty young boys frolicked on the big "field" in front of the house. It always just went by the name "field".

Before sitting down at table we had had a round with Max. It often happened that we did this and everyone knew what it was all about. It was a fight with everyone against one and one against everyone. Max was, of course, the one. Regardless of how many we were, we had to try to get him on the ground, while him, using every trick in the book, and those he had many of, had to stay on his feet.

At times it became a bit rough, with nosebleeds and abrasions, but there were never any serious injuries and I must add that as far as I recall, we never managed to get him on the ground.

What he had acquired of personal attack and defence techniques during his *training as a saboteur in England, one could probably write thick books about, and they probably exist in vast numbers.*

Those in the "everyone" group laid, as always, scattered across the "field" after he, with the speed of lightning, had easily feinted us all away, one or several at a time.

I don't know what Max did when we went to sit down at the table and I never gave it a second thought, there were after all sausages and birthday cake to be had. Stuffed and happy, and after being bored with football, Cowboys and Indians took over. Being Indian was the least popular so, as usual, it was the "eenie meenie" method which decided who would be what and this usually went well as long as no one got caught cheating during the "eenie meenie".

As already mentioned, there was a lot of wooded area on the property, so there were a lot of places to hide.

I had just moved from the main house and been given a room with my own entrance in the middle house. I remember it well as being more than twenty square meters and as long as it was wide.

In the corner just inside the door on the right stood the bed, and in the opposite corner a modern, in those days, cast iron fire place. Below the window next to the bed was a desk and chair.

The rest of the house was inhabited by our housekeeper and nanny. The latter had been employed as a result of my half-brother and half-sister being born in 1947 and 1949 respectively and because my mother worked as Max's secretary at the office in Oslo.

My thoughts were on completely different matters than on Max. I knew, however, that he was going to take part in some National Guard manoeuvres that evening and night, but that was a completely natural situation for him at the weekends.

He was the leader of the National Guard in Asker and had early on introduced realistic exercises.

That these exercises were realistic there's no doubt about. I recall very well that he once combined such an exercise with something which served his purpose.

The apple orchard at Norderhaug, mentioned in the introduction, was divided into two parts, the upper one and the lower one. The lower one started directly behind the main house and went as far as the outhouse, about one hundred meters from the house. The trees in the lower part of the garden were ancient, at least those which were close to the house and they were probably ripe for replacement as they didn't produce much fruit. I don't know if this was the actual motive, but enough said.

A special unit of the National Guard was to be trained in explosives technique and thus it was that one apple tree after the other blew up with a deafening boom. The charges were placed at different heights on the trunks so that they afterwards could study the effects. After that the charges were buried below the roots so that they became part of the volleys. To have cut down the trees and later removed the roots a different way would have been a very complicated and time-consuming job.

This wasn't the first time there were complaints from the neighbours, but it was seldom they came as far away as from Øvre Nes Manor, which I would estimate to be situated more then a kilometre away to the north across the valley.

This was a bit of side-tracking with hardly any reflex but it hopefully provides a bit of background information to what happened later on this birthday.

I can't remember what lead up to it, but there was probably something I wanted to fetch in my room.

I run up the steps to the porch from which the door led straight into my room. As I grab the door handle and start to open the door, a shadowy presence moves at the speed of lightning from the bed diagonally across to the fire place, a good distance from the floor.

It seemed to me that it happened before the door was fully opened.

When I've pulled myself together after the shock, I see Max standing, totally confused, with his back to the fire place in a position which made it seem like he had a weapon in his hand, which I hasten to add that he did not. I was already at the time fully informed about firing positions.

He practised constantly, either in the garden or at the shooting range, and I almost always came along. When he came to a moment later, he reacted with rage, but this abated as soon as he understood that I hadn't woken him on purpose.

What I described as a shadowy presence was of course Max, but can my impression really be correct, that he actually made a four meter jump from the bed to the fire place?

He had gone in there to have a good rest before the military manoeuvres he was to lead the same night, as far away from our meal and subsequent football as possible and hadn't expected to be disturbed.

I can only speculate as to what took place in his sub consciousness as he lay there sleeping prior to my grabbing the door handle and his making his reflex reaction the way he did. One thing is clear, however, it wasn't the office which was on his mind.

The Barn

In several of these stories from Landøya the barn has been mentioned. Red roof tiles, standing red-painted panel on the exterior walls and white ridges and window frames. The stacking loft was exciting and was frequently used to play in on dark winter days when the weather was not too tempting.

All this applied to the first few years after the war only, for as long as the stacking loft continued to be exciting. What we played, I barely remember, but that we at times put extra grey hairs on the heads of the Bergstrøms there is little doubt about.

Anyway, more and more of the stuff which couldn't be placed in the main house or the middle house, was stacked in the barn.

Long after I moved from Landøya and had my own family and home, I also ended up placing different things there as we moved from our apartment in Halvdan Svartesgate and on to Skillebekk. Apart from this I had gradually acquired a not insignificant collection of antique typewriters; this as a result of my special interest in their technical aspects and my having worked for several years on the development of various typewriter concepts. These I had no room for at home, so they were put in the barn awaiting further plans.

Max was constantly thinking of tearing down the barn with an eye to building a new house for him and my mother, so that the main house would be available for the next generation.

The plans must have taken shape and made a breakthrough because at one point he started nagging me about getting rid of what I over time had accumulated up there in the barn.

Being very busy in connection with both business and leisure activities, I didn't pay much attention to these requests, something I later regretted. Their plans must have become reality. The barn had undoubtedly the best location on the entire property in that it was situated on the upper part of it, with a nice view down towards both the middle and the main house and between the treetops one could look northwards across the valley all the way to the Nes Manor. It was the perfect place on the property to build the new house.

It was probably in connection with their having been given approval of the plans to build what, when it was completed, was to be called the "Tower House" that the demolition plans were suddenly speeded up. The Bergstrøms had moved out several years before, so everything was ready to go.

This is where my memory gets a bit confused. I remember well that Max on several occasions had mentioned that he had plans to arrange a National Guard exercise aiming to burn down the barn. I assume the materials in themselves were of little value and that it would cost more to do an organized demolition than to burn the whole thing. The time must have flown relatively quickly, however, as I understand from more reliable family sources than myself in this context, that Max was no longer leader of the National Guard when the barn was torn down.

Thus the original plan could not be implemented.

Meanwhile, a man called Magnar was living in the middle house. He was in the process of starting up a business of his own and had acquired an excavator. He and his friend Vidar were thus given as one of their first jobs, the task of tearing down the barn, prior to doing all the digging connected with the "Tower House".

Everything had been well prepared I believe and even though there is something not quite certain about the details, the Asker fire brigade was probably called in to stand by for that which was to be the start of the demolition, namely a fire. No one can verify the truth of this, but what is certain is that when Magnar was to light the fire of the barn itself, it came close to being a catastrophe. For unknown reasons petrol had been spilled and he was only a hair's breadth from being reduced to ashes himself.

After the fire itself, which seems to have gone well and been successful in every way, Magnar's excavator took over. He crushed that which was left standing and there's no doubt about the entire process having been precise and efficient, for that which remained at the end could be removed in just a few lorry loads.

It might be that I was given a last warning to remove those of my belongings that I wanted to keep, as they would otherwise disappear in the heat of the battle, but regardless, it didn't happen in time.

Among the burnt wreckage there must have been just over a dozen destroyed antique typewriters, as well as prototypes of parts belonging to our own electromechanical typewriter, which unfortunately never got to be displayed in any museum, but that's nobody's fault but mine. The demolition of the barn itself took place in the summer of 1980 and thanks to Magnar's skills and excavator, the foundations of that which, after a reasonable amount of construction time, was to be the "Tower House", drawn by the architect, Odd Jebe, went very well. All of it happened to the delight of the female part of the next generation, who then took over the main house.

The Garage

It was perhaps not so strange that there was no garage at Landøya when we moved there. The garage had, of course, been invented, but the few cars which existed in the area before the war and the very few which were still running immediately after the war, meant that the need to have a separate house for them, was very limited.

Max had, however, from the very first day we moved in, got hold of a Mercedes convertible. If I had wanted to do some research into the matter, I could probably have found out which model it was, but for me that's not necessary. I believe there are family films and photos of it and whenever I want, I can conjure up the memory of my grandfather sitting on his own in the back seat of this jet black streamlined star edition with its top down, during a pit stop, either to or from Lærdal where he lived. If it's my grandfather or the car which is strongest in my memory, I can't say for sure, perhaps they are equally strong, when all is said and done. Endurance and durability combined with quality on all fronts.

However, at this time just after the war, there was a challenge on the mechanical side as far as spare parts were concerned as not only were the parts difficult to come by, but in most cases they were impossible to obtain.

Max was a typical handyman, who fixed most things of a mechanical character on his own and had a great imagination when it came to finding improvised solutions. Playing the mechanic in summer was no problem but in winter it was quite different, in snow, wind and bitter cold, if there was no roof over one's head.

As a natural consequence of this, he already during the late autumn of the first post-war year got help with putting up a provisional roof in front of the entrance to the main house, between it and a wall which formed the border to the elevated breakfast place next to the big chestnut tree. This became a parking space for the Mercedes combined with our workshop.

Perhaps not in the most appropriate place, as we all had to go through this unfinished space in order to get into the main house.

The latter was probably part of Max's plans as it must have been no later than the following spring when he started work on building a proper garage with sufficient space for two cars and a mechanic's pit high enough to stand up in. Åsmund Jørgensen, a close relative of fisher Jørgensen, the one with the sausages, was given responsibility for the rough work.

Seen from the gate towards the middle house, the garage was to be situated to the right. The hill ran steeply from the non-excavated first floor of the middle house and up towards the level of its living quarters.

The excavation must at the time have been fairly extensive and I can't recall an excavator or anything similar being used. It must have been done using a wheel barrow, hoe and spade, and then taking everything away on a lorry.

Gradually an extensive formwork was created with support beams which would hold the flat concrete roof in place, while the reinforcement strengthened after the cement dried.

At the front of the garage, Åsmund had put together a large square box, which I assume must have been about three times three meters and a little less than a meter high. Here the cement would be mixed. There was, of course, no such thing as a cement mixer in those days. It was done by Åsmund standing in the middle of the "pen" while his helper poured in sand and cement, which he then mixed with water using a spade.

If the ready-mixed cement was then brought around and up in a wheel barrow or was hoisted up, I don't remember, but since it was all done manually the filling of the forms took a seemingly long time even though extra help was called in.

At the time I, of course, didn't understand that the building material concrete was a mixture of cement, sand and perhaps stones and water. Åsmund had late in the afternoon emptied the "pen" of that day's ready-mixed cement and got everything set up for the next day. Cement in the right proportion to sand he had already mixed in large quantities with the aid of hundreds of digs with his spade, to get an easier start the following day. All that was needed was the right amount of water, renewed mixing with the spade and it would all be ready for transport to the forms.

I choose in retrospect to believe that I meant to give Åsmund a helping hand, not commit sabotage, which is what it looked like the next day when Åsmund arrived for the day's work. Or, could it be possible that I already understood the process and did it on purpose? Anyway, I have already admitted to not being an angel, but could I really have been that bl...y bad?

I had worn myself out the evening before, filling the "pen" with water, probably even with some help from my friends too. The next morning Åsmund was greeted by a solid lump of concrete measuring more than one cubic meter the next morning.

I don't remember what my punishment consisted of, so it's quite possible that the whole thing was seen as my wanting to "give a helping hand", although I doubt it.

The garage was gradually finished and was frequently used as home to a lot of different cars which the family acquired as time went by.

My first car, a Lancia Aprilia 1949 model, which I bought in Italy while going to school there, went through a complete change of rod bearings with me as a mechanic, standing in the "pit".

I must add that immediately after the garage was finished, the provisional one in front of the entrance to the main house was removed, not least to the relief of my mother.

Both the foundation, the walls and the flat roof, all in concrete, must have been ever so solid, as only a few years later an apartment was built on top of it.

It, which can be called an extension of the middle house as both its roof and ridge is an extension of the same, is still there and was my mother's dwelling the last few years of her life until she died at the age of 96.

Explanation

What's inside me can't be explained with words of sound -
even though my feet are planted on the ground.
The meaning of words, what they're meant to portray -
must never become locked or fixed in any way.
The courage of our convictions we must have and express -
as only thus we can find happiness.
GM

That's what I've always said

September 2012

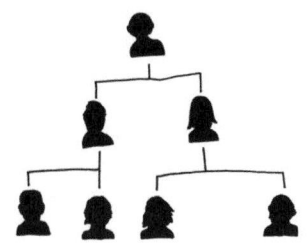

How often hasn't one heard this phrase? "That's what I've always said" or "that's what I've always thought". Said or thought is more or less the same for what I infer about these expressions.

Regardless, they stem, after my opinion, from that part of the population who are "followers" or "hangers on". These expressions are seldom or never heard from leaders.

I should have dealt with this subject 20 or 30 years ago, at the time when I, just for myself and no one else, analysed this and other similar expressions.

Now, many years later, this reflection probably won't be as accurate as it would have been had I put it to paper in those days.

Time takes the edge off things and black and white become shades of grey.

The wrong man or woman in the wrong place isn't discovered too easily until one sees the result of their work.

We're talking more about middle management here, not about top leaders and certainly not about those at the shop floor level.

A top leader would never use the above mentioned expressions. Not because he or she is consciously not using them, but because such expressions don't belong to their nature.

Seen from the point of view of a top leader it's quite simple, if you've "always said it" or "thought it for some time", then you've obviously already done something about it, in other words, it's a challenge long gone.

I don't in any way want to discriminate against middle management, but I'm afraid my own experience shows that it's just here that most of the challenges in business lie.

It is where the battles of competence, prestige and position are fought.

Where the strategies made by top management are put into practice and implemented throughout the organization.

The interpretation of the message is never perceived the same way and thus implemented differently. The technical staff for instance, hasn't got the same mindset for interpreting the message as the commercial staff, or the other way around, and certainly not after the message has been chewed over by middle management and been given their various slants.

That was obviously quite a mouthful, so I'll get back to the expressions.

When unintended consequences triggered by leadership have to be put right, it is seldom or never the so-called shop floor person who is to blame. On the contrary, those in question probably has a very clear idea of what their work entails and what is expected of them, and an attack here probably ends the same way as when the errand boy in the old days gave his bicycle a kick of frustration caused by his interpretation of the instructions or attitude of his boss.

This last statement probably has no meaning for a lot of people, as what is an errand boy in today's world?

Here it is middle management, those there are normally too many of, who come under fire.

Why there are too many cooks as a rule and the broth gets spoiled lies, in my opinion, in the nature of things.

I hasten to add that my experiences as a leader go back 10 to 15 or many more years and that one today is probably much further ahead when it comes to these types of business challenges.

In those days people didn't change jobs as often as one changes one's shirt. There was something called loyalty to one's firm. The employees remained in the firm, and positions were "created" for them which quite often were somewhat artificial.

One looked at seniority and experience to a greater extent than at more rational things such as basic education combined with length of employment and skills.

This often resulted in an unnaturally large number of middle management, which didn't exactly contribute to decreasing the challenges.

No one must misunderstand me and think that I don't believe that many, also today, have a strong sense of loyalty toward the company they work for, but development has created other values.

With the middle management under fire, questions were often asked as

138

to why this or that hadn't happened in such and such a way and whether the person concerned didn't agree with those decisions taken by the top management; moreover it was considered whether the person concerned understood that it was his or her responsibility to put the decisions into practice.

The answer when it came, somewhat in despair, was that it had been perfectly understood and "that's what I've always said and thought".

In other words, there was no lack of loyalty and agreement, but of the ability to implement.

Since it is precisely the ability to implement which is the responsibility of middle management, one understands that when this kind of reply is given, the wrong person has been given the position of leadership.

The "follower" or "hanger on" is, of course, also entitled to a job, but not as a responsible leader.

Another and far more important aspect of all this, is that it is the top management's responsibility to put the right person in middle management.

As I've already mentioned, had I dealt with this subject 20 or more years ago, the content would probably have been presented more clearly, but my attitude to the challenge would have been the same.

Gossip

The words that wander from mouth to ear -
can for some be sad to hear.
So let the thoughts in your mind go around,
before you commit them to paper or sound.
GM

The Breithorn

November 2012

Going by train from Oslo to Milan in 1956 to be schooled in the little town of Ivrea at the bottom of the Aosta valley in Northern Italy, my slalom skis were among my travelling companions.

I was 17 years old and had been told that there were excellent skiing possibilities just an hour's drive from where I would stay.

It was a long journey with two nights on the same train. Why this preamble, well, because the export manager for Scandinavia, representing Olivetti, the office equipment factory we were agents for in Norway, and who was to be my mentor during my stay at the school, himself was a former alpine guide.

Since we already knew each other well from his many visits to our home and because he knew I was a keen skier, he had on several occasions said that he would be happy to take me skiing when it suited me.

His name was, Dinko Podkrajsek, which is probably not the right spelling.

I believe he was originally from Yugoslavia, but even that I'm not quite sure of. He died more than 20 years ago.

The episode I want to talk about took place the following spring, in May if I remember correctly, in other words in 1957. It has remained for several reasons unforgettable.

The usual starting point of Dinko's excursions into the mountains was the little village of Champoluc, located in a side valley on the way up from Valle d'Aosta at one end of the nowadays well-known ski resort area, Monte Rosa, at the time about a two-hour drive from Ivrea.

We mustn't forget that this happened 55 years ago and that the motorway which today runs through the entire valley, the St. Bernard tunnel and into Switzerland didn't exist. He himself had a very charming, little cabin up there, but for a short week-end stay it was easier to book in at one of the local hotels.

We stayed there on several occasions and I seem to remember that its name was Hotel Rosa. It was a small intimate hotel run by a husband and wife.

If it was he or she who was in charge of the kitchen, I don't remember but it was certainly magnificent those times we sat in the little restaurant with its crackling fire and delicious home-cooked food accompanied by a lovely Barolo red wine from Piemonte.

I had understood from the very first moment of my stay that wine with the food was obligatory and part of Italian culture. It's strange how adaptable one is when one is young. The same applied to the language.

After only a month, having been placed in a class where only Italian was spoken, it also became natural that all communication from my side should haltingly take place in the local language, albeit with total disrespect for grammar.

The packing of everything needed for our expedition the next day, as well as getting our skis and all other equipment ready, was done immediately after dinner as we, in order to make the trip in one day, according to Dinko, had to leave before sunrise.

The weather forecast was apparently good so everything should be in our favour.

He had probably told me where we were going, but I hadn't paid too much attention. I didn't know the area well anyway, so my knowledge of our destination didn't matter too much.

What I had registered was that we from the altitude of Champoluc at 450 meters above sea level would work our way up to somewhere above 4,000 meters, which meant a difference in altitude of somewhat less than 4 kilometres.

If I remember correctly there was only a limited amount of ski-lifts in Champoluc in those days, and since the skiing season was over, we wouldn't be able to use any of them anyway. Aside from that, we were also starting out several hours before any of them would have opened.

With a beautiful deep blue sky above us, the sun had yet to wake up let alone rise, we set off up the mountain with our skis on our shoulders. There was no snow in the area; we were after all well into May.

We could, of course, see the white-capped mountaintops high up there in the distance, these being our only connection with winter apart from the skis which we could feel on our shoulders after only a short time.

We walked parallel to and crossed quite a few creeks filled with water cascading at great speed down the mountainside, as if competing with one another in reaching the Dora, the main river running through Valle d'Aosta.

It, by the way, ran just past my window, where I was staying at Hotel Dora in Ivrea, before joining the river Po on it's long trip towards the Adriatic Sea.

We're surrounded by green and it undeniably feels a bit un-Norwegian to be trudging up the steep mountainside with slalom skis dressed in seal skin on one's shoulders in amongst mooing cows.

We stop at regular intervals to slake our thirst with the crystal clear water from the creeks before we again continue our upward trek.

The last of the farms are finally left behind and from now on there is only nature on all sides. After a while the landscape flattens out somewhat but continues its upward slope.

Surrounding us on all sides, the valley we've climbed, having disappeared, we see imposing snow-covered mountain ranges, with their characteristic peaks, known by name only to those familiar with the area.

The sun having had a nourishing breakfast is bursting with energy against a Mediterranean blue sky.

Our first rest takes place when we at last reach the first patches of snow.

I'll never forget how we settled ourselves in front of the stone ruins of an old Mountain farm, to have our breakfast.

Snowy patches, which still hadn't given up their impossible fight against the embrace of pre-summer, were scattered all around, covering larger or smaller bits of ground, and sunglasses had to be put on.

I believe I forgot to say that even before leaving the hotel, Dinko insisted on the two of us putting on masks of sun protection cream. It wasn't a question of just slapping a bit of cream in our faces; no, both ears and necks had to be carefully covered. It felt like wearing a stiff plaster mask which covered one's entire head apart from where the cap was.

With my lack of experience with anything other than normal sun cream while skiing in Norway, I thought this went a bit too far, but he was the boss after all.

Up to now our white faces had made a contrast to all the green but now, surrounded by scattered patches of snow, we seemed, at least facially, to blend in more with our surroundings.

Another and far more interesting colour contrast is the one which on this trip glued itself into the scrapbook.

Only now as I'm writing about the event, have I looked in the reference books to find the name of the flower I could see in great quantities between the patches of snow and which made such an unforgettable impression on me.

This incredibly beautiful flower which I'm referring to is called Gentian, in Latin, Gentiana Brachyphylla. Its blue colour can't be described accurately; it has to be experienced in those surroundings where nature has let it adorn the landscape.

Its radiance and colour contrasting with the white snow-covered mountaintops is a diamond among nature experiences and is apparently to be found only in these settings.

I admit that cyclamen in different colours are also magnificent in their surroundings but even though 22 different species are to be found, they can't compete with the species of the Gentian family which I experienced at that time.

What particular species of the 400 family members it was, I won't try to research, but I believe it must have been the Gentiana Verna or Spring Gentian. I believe they can grow at an altitude up to 2,600 meters.

Yes, even the Edelweiss, the Lion's Paw, doesn't surpass it in beauty.

After having enjoyed both the provisions we'd brought along and the beautiful surroundings, a good stretch remained before we could strap on our skis.

The kandahar ski bindings and the seal skins, together with the so-called ''beksømstøvler", welt boots stitched with pitch-covered thread, which were normally worn in those days, made it possible to move upwards in relative comfort, even on the steepest slopes.

Now all we had to do was enjoy the experience. The rucksacks were not too heavy, so it was all in all a wonderful experience of nature.

The sun was on its way up too, just like we were.

Our first goal was to reach the glacier which I believe he called Plateau Rosa.

The word Rosa has in this context nothing to do with either the colour or the flower, but simply means glacier.

When Rosa is used as the name of a hotel, it doesn't normally have to do with either a glacier or a colour, but the rose itself.

Anyway, I'm not at all sure that this is correct.

We finally reach a plateau which looks like a frozen lake covered in snow. I can't say anything about its size but in my memory it seems like a never-ending flat plain. The sub-goal has been reached, this is Plateau Rosa.

From here on Dinko got out a climbing rope which he insisted that we, one at each end, fasten around our waists. In other words, we suddenly became two tied-together people with a maximum distance of about 10 meters between us.

Was he afraid of bad weather despite the beautiful cloudless sky? Could the fog suddenly take us by surprise?

He didn't offer any explanation, just told me to wait and see.

Earlier on we had taken turns making tracks but now there were no questions asked, he was in the lead.

The reflection from the intense sun which was now directly above us on the enormous white plain, convinces me that without the earlier mentioned protection, we would have been fried alive. Now, on the other hand, the mask felt like a necessary and natural cooling factor.

We move forward on the thin layer of snow with the aid of our sticks and turn slowly towards the right, which I believe must have been the northern end of the plateau.

Dinko suddenly stops and beckons me towards him. It takes me only a few seconds to get there and he says something like: Now you will see why we are tied together. With the ice axe, which he has hanging on his rucksack; he bends down and hits the snow in front of him. A boom is heard and suddenly the snow is gone at a width of about half a meter and a length of fifty to a hundred meters. Everything happens in just a few seconds and all we can see down the crevice are two ice-blue walls for as far as the sunlight reaches and then it becomes pitch black.

My heart skips several beats before I see Dinko remove his skis asking me to remain where I am. He then throws them to the other side of the crevice and he himself jumps across.

Not to dramatize, I again state that the crevice was only about half a meter wide, but when he asks me to do the same, I follow with my heart in my throat. He didn't need to elaborate further on why we were tied together.

We quickly approach the edge of the plateau, from where the white surface just continues upwards until it, way up high, contrasting with the blue sky, forms the top of the Breithorn in all its width.

On our left we've seen for some time the characteristic silhouette of the Matterhorn which, unlike the Breithorn's height of 4,165 meters, rises 4,478 meters above sea level and is considered the sixth most difficult mountain in the world to climb.

The Breithorn, our goal, is on the other hand considered one of the easiest.

At a distance it was difficult to see where the plateau ended and the mountain began, but when we got closer it was easy to spot.

The skis now had to give way to an attack just in boots.

These were encased in a sort of climbing shoe of steel so that we wouldn't lose our footing.

I see when I examine the details, that the upward slope is about 35 degrees.

It doesn't sound very steep, but I can assure the readers that it felt quite different at the time. It seemed as if we were about to climb a white wall.

With the rope safely anchored between us and the ice axe in Dinko's right hand, we moved slowly but surely upwards, one step at a time, in the axe marks he made in the almost ice-hard snow.

I crawled more than stood up straight, already feeling that this was not my element. But there was no question of showing weakness; a sissy from Norway wasn't how I wanted to be remembered after an excursion like this one.

I quickly lost track of time as it was hard enough keeping up with Dinko's rhythmical attack on the mountainside.

How long the climb lasted, from Plateau Rosa to the top, I have no recollection of from the time, but I see now that the plateau lies at 3,480 meters. The ascent is, in other words, 685 meters with a 35 degree gradient. Even now, in retrospect, I have no idea how long the ascent took.

Suddenly I can see Dinko as a silhouette against the sky.

He has chopped away the top layer of ice and made a little plateau which he is standing on. Just the sight of him standing there totally at ease looking around, almost makes me throw up.

After having pulled myself seriously together, bent forward practically lying there with my face near the icy snow, I get out my camera and take a picture which I still think I have as a keepsake.

I now see quite clearly that from where Dinko is standing there are only two ways to descend, the one we've just come up and the other straight down into Switzerland.

As effortlessly as possible, I move the last 8 to 10 meters slightly more upright than before and when I reach the summit in front of his feet, I throw my right leg across so that I end up sitting, or perhaps lying astride the ridge itself.

Even if I was sitting at the start, it didn't last many seconds, as I the very next moment looked straight down into Zermatt in Switzerland, my face making instant contact with the ice.

Everyone knows that it isn't literally straight down, but it seems that way, at a drop of two and a half kilometres, Zermatt lies at 1,600 meters.

I remain lying like that for a while before pulling myself together. In the same lying down position my camera is slowly fumbled forth and another picture of Dinko is taken, standing up.

To my question if he won't sit down, he answers that he enjoys the view better standing up.

What if I start sliding down the side? I ask.

No problem is the answer, then I just let myself slide down the other side, which is one of the reasons we're tied together.

It was at this moment I realized for the first time what a fear of heights means, and it has stayed with me and is just as strong today as when I first discovered it that day on top of the Breithorn.

As long as we stayed at the top, I didn't budge. Just lay in the same position the whole time, but little by little I managed to get control over my nerves and take in the magnificent surroundings.

It was a lot easier to look along the ridge of the Breithorn and up onto the Matterhorn than down into Zermatt.

The way down followed the same tracks Dinko had made with his axe on the way up, but this time with myself in the lead, backwards with my face plastered to the icy surface, and himself behind with the rope held taut.

Back down on the plateau, we took a break where the skis stood and where the impressions could be digested along with the packed lunch.

It was already quite late in the afternoon.

There can be no doubt that Dinko had fully realized that the tough and, at times, big mouthed, young Norwegian skier had learnt a lesson when it came to experiences of this kind and that he in future would show more respect for nature.

We then went farther across the Plateau in the direction of Cervinia which lies at about two thousand meters. In other words, we had to go down about another fifteen hundred meters.

Wonderful thoughts as we were getting ready after having stowed away the seal skins in our rucksacks. Ahead of us lay the skiing highlight of the day.

I had earlier been to Cervinia and taken the lift up to Plateau Rosa to ski down the trail which at the time was used among other things for competitions in Speed Skiing.

With egg-shaped helmets and special suits and skis, this is the world's most rapid sport on earth without the use of an engine. Today, the record, which is measured over 100 meters in the middle of the track at up to a 45 degree gradient, is more than 250 kilometres an hour.

For us it went quite fast, but I doubt that we even reached half of that speed.

Having reached Cervinia, we were met by a friend of Dinko's who had driven there from Champoluc to pick us up.

Being reasonably exhausted after the day's efforts, it was for me a drive during which the impressions of nature gave way to dreaming about the day's events. The evening itself and the dinner at Hotel Rosa, I don't remember anything about, the impressions of the day had been too strong.

As one can appreciate, I'm badly equipped for mountain climbing.

I have had a great number of wonderful skiing experiences in beautiful surroundings later in life both in Norway, Switzerland and Austria, but nothing can ever compare with this May day with Dinko, when we climbed the Breithorn.

The Chin

November 2012

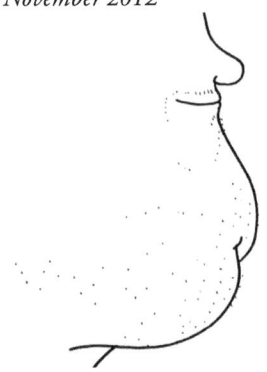

In the Norwegian expression "hva er haken ved det", the word "haken" translates as "the chin" but if it has anything to do with the chin I'm thinking of, I don't know.

Doesn't the expression mean something like "what's the drawback/problem with that"? I don't know, but if that's the case, then the chin, the one I'm thinking of, ought to have something to do with drawbacks/problems.

Well, it might be interesting to have a look at that some time. Couldn't stop myself, had to do a bit of checking. Eureka, in English the expression is: "what's the catch", in other words, easy to associate with "hook", the one which has to do with fishing or hunting, not the one in golf.

Now things are starting to come together. Of course, it has to do with the sort of hook used to catch one's prey. In English it becomes quite clear, for what does a "hooker" do but catch her man?

In other words, this type of catch or hook has nothing to do with my chin.

That the chin I'm about to tackle is placed in the lower part of one's face, below the mouth, has by now become clear to everyone. Why it's there and what its uses are, I won't go into yet, let's just chew on it.

I assume only a few know the answers, for if one goes into Wikipedia one has to make do with my description, in other words, that it is placed in the lower part of one's face, below the mouth.

As if we don't all know that. Has anyone ever seen a chin placed above the mouth? That would look absurd, as that's where the nose is, so how would the chin fit?

I have to admit though, that Wikipedia goes a bit further by saying that a cleft chin is hereditary. That's also something one doesn't have to be too intelligent to understand, most of us know the Douglases as an example, both the father, Kirk, and the son, Michael. The father was born in 1916 and the son in 1944. Even though Kirk was born, Issur Danielovitch, and was Russian, they're a good example of the hereditariness of the cleft chin. The phenomenon is sure to lie not only in Russian genes.

Regardless, nature doesn't normally equip us with parts which haven't got special or defined roles.

It is clear that our lower teeth are hinged to the upper ones so that we can chew, but wouldn't it then have been sufficient with a solid platform in the lower part of the mouth from where our teeth could grow?

No, that would have been too simple; the tongue's importance in the middle of everything carries a heavy weight in this respect.

Just try to move your tongue with your mouth closed and feel how much room it has in which to move about. The movement of the tongue is significant to the formation of what we say. By this, I mean the sounds that are produced, not what is being said, as that of course, is determined by the brain.

We are now a bit further in explaining the reason for having a chin.

But why isn't it more similar from person to person?

Some have a pronounced chin, the type which protrudes, often past the mouth. Some haven't got a chin at all, but when this happens to men, they often grow a becoming beard to remedy the matter.

The same reason but with a different denominator make men with an undershot bite, that's when the lower teeth protrude in front of the upper ones, grow a moustache in order to maintain what is probably considered a suitable profile.

Don't misunderstand me by thinking that every time one sees a moustache or a beard, the person has had the above reasons for growing them, far from it.

Yes, there's suddenly a lot to consider.

I have never dwelt on to what degree women are concerned about their chins.

They are usually concerned about themselves, for which we men should be grateful. It probably varies like everything else, to what extent women are concerned with their chins, but when I asked my wife about it in connection with this reflection she seemed to think that in her everyday life, she's not especially concerned about hers.

It is, however, not especially protruding and doesn't form part of that which each morning is given special attention in front of the mirror.

She also didn't say that she paid any special attention to a man's chin, but that it should be in proportion to the other parts of his face.

She did, however, add that she was glad not to have a "protruding" chin, so she seems to be a bit concerned about it after all.

Enough said. I'll stop this here as I could otherwise end up on thin ice and risk giving offence.

Isn't there something about a strong chin representing decisiveness and the opposite a not so decisive and more hesitant attitude?

Regardless of whether it's correct or not, and whatever the reader thinks, it's probably not that simple.

That it's determined by the appearance of the whole face is probably closer to the truth.

Does for instance a big nose relate to a strong chin or do they fight for dominance.

Now there's even more to think about.

As regards the information about the chin, I haven't looked anywhere else but Wikipedia, it might be that other encyclopaedias have more detailed information.

I don't want to be the judge of it myself, but I'm personally quite satisfied with both my nose and my chin and since my mother repeatedly told me during my adolescence that she didn't think much of hairy faces, as she called it, I grew up as an obedient son and have never had a beard or a moustache.

It probably can't be as simple as that, but my mother divorced my father, her first husband, at an early stage, and he was English and had a moustache.

Not too much greed and not too much spending
not too aggressive or too defending.
Not too evil and not too good
this is what I have understood.
GM

The Conductor

September 2010

There's something very special about a conductor. Not the one conducting traffic, even though that has been turned into an artistic performance by some.

In English a conductor can also be someone who sells tickets on trains and buses just like a "konduktør" in Norway.

That's also not who I'm thinking about, however. That profession is in any case, at least in Norway, dying out due to automation.

It is the person who coordinates, inspires and intones, in short, the one who via an orchestra or choir delivers a personally wrapped presentation of a composer's piece of music or song to the audience.

What makes one conductor better than the other shall remain unsaid, but it is incredible for an outsider to see how totally most of them immerse themselves into the music during a performance.

Their personality, the charisma itself, is of special value for the inspiration and thus the musical expression of the musicians. The rhythm and pace is determined entirely by the conductor.

I have always admired them for their unbelievable knowledge of music and the musical abilities that they must have.

One always pictures the conductor with a baton in his hand.

Why a baton is called "taktstokk" in Norwegian I don't know as it would be more natural to call it a "taktpinne" since a "pinne-pin"is much thinner than a "stokk", but I believe it originally has something to do with the "takt" or time originally being kept by tapping a "stokk" or stick on the floor.

The word 'baton' in English, I apologize for the digression, can also refer to a stick or club of greater dimensions such as the ones used by the police to keep demonstrators under control, and this definitely has nothing to do with a "pinne".

I suppose we just have to accept reality and not go too deeply into such insignificant details.

It was only after 1850 that it became normal for an orchestra to be led by a conductor. Before that, the task was given to one of the leading instrumentalists in the orchestra itself.

The excitement can really be felt when an entire symphony orchestra has finished tuning and the conductor enters the stage and gets up onto the podium.

It's probably not his or her status which puts him or her on a higher level than at least the nearest instruments, but the necessity of his or her being seen by the musicians.

He or she is after all the conductor and must been seen by everyone.

There seem to be a lot of he or she descriptions here, but one shall not discriminate. Percentage-wise there are probably a lot fewer female conductors than male ones, but they exist and are sure to be just as proficient at their jobs as their male colleagues.

After the initial applause, the first few seconds before the baton is raised, are characterized by total silence, then the music starts with a vengeance. This is not always the case, of course, as sometimes a few humble notes can be the start of a great masterpiece.

I've noted that the conductor of a choir seldom or never uses a baton; at least I've never seen it. One normally sees this conductor, who doesn't use any other tool but himself, seemingly singing along, but if his voice can be heard, I can't say as I've never been able to tell.

I myself have no musical background. My mother on the other hand played the piano in her youth and wanted me to have lessons, something which I have always regretted not having done.

In my mature years, however, I have become quite fond of classical music and enjoy both opera and ballet.

Not that I delve into the detailed lives of composers and performers, but the joy and good feeling which comes from listening to classical music are always there.

Since we live in the south of Spain, however, it is unfortunately seldom that we get to attend live musical performances. On the other hand, we enjoy among others, Spanish TV2, which especially on Saturday mornings show concerts of all kinds, from complete symphony orchestras to the more humble chamber variety.

In the car, the radio is always tuned to the Spanish Radio Classica.

During my school years in Italy I had an experience which I only in retrospect came to understand as quite special.

I had the fortune to be invited to La Scala in Milan to see Puccini's Manon Lescaut.

I had just turned 17 and was more interested in girls than in opera and classical music in general, but it sounded interesting.

I don't remember any details from the performance itself, but the atmosphere was ecstatic from the start. I believe Herbert Von Karajan swung the baton and Maria Callas sang Manon Lescaut.

It must have been a fantastic and probably unique experience for connoisseurs, but I must admit that I at that time didn't understand how unique the performance was. Later on, however, I have realized that I must have witnessed one of the absolute highlights within the genre.

After having written "The Conductor" and made reference to my visit to La Scala, I have been in doubt as to whether I really saw Callas and Karajan in the same performance. During my stay in Italy I visited La Scala twice and I have to admit that I may be a bit confused as it was, after all, 55 years ago.

I therefore consulted my brother who is a know-it-all as regards these things.

It ended up confusing me even more, however, as I was presented with all the Callas performances in the years 56 and 57 and with different conductors. I have thus chosen to leave things as they are as regards this episode.

Is it something I imagine or is there usually something special about the hairstyle of male conductors? It appears to be either frizzy or wild, or long, and sometimes in a ponytail. Anyway, it seems to me as if most of them have lots of hair.

I haven't noticed anything special about the hairdos of female conductors, however.

As far as I can tell, it's only the pianists who are fortunate enough to have someone turn the pages of their scores as the music progresses.

All the other instrumentalists must do it themselves and this is where I feel it becomes somewhat special. Just imagine, someone as elevated as the conductor, the boss himself, isn't privileged enough to merit a "page-turning slave". Perhaps the offer is there, but he himself chooses to stand on his own two feet?

Only once have I seen a conductor sitting down while conducting. He was, however, 98 years old and from Valencia, and he did have a "page-turning slave" sitting next to him.

So excited and impressed by conductors am I that I a while back bought a print by the, somewhat special but by now quite well-known, Norwegian artist, Pushwagner, who in my opinion does the best rendering of a conductor giving his all during a performance.

Strength

When we talk about strength, we think about steel
but it can also appear like the softest eel.
When heated, things take on a different form
and thus make changes to the current norm.
GM

The Driving Licence
May 2013

I can't remember there being such a thing as a driving licence at the time when I was a candidate for getting my "certificate" as it was then called, but that's beside the point. Regardless, driving licence is a more precise term for the document which gives you the right to drive a car; it leaves no doubt as to what it is. A certificate can refer to so many things. A bit of background information is once again needed in order to understand what the following is all about.

My stepfather, Max, must in many ways have been a perfect father figure, not that I only saw his positive traits, but one thing is certain, he never held back when it came to giving me freedom with responsibility. This freedom I've always cherished and as far as I know, it has seldom, at least not consciously, been abused.

In connection with my driving licence started in an, at least nowadays, non-traditional way. I believe it must have been in 1947 that my mother was given her Morris Minor. It was most unusual in those days, in Norway, to be able to buy any new car other than a Moskvich from Russia even the purchasing licences were hard to come by. Max, however, had earned some money in England, as a result of his war books having been published there, so getting a licence seemed to be no problem.

A few years went by before I got to give it a try, but it's certain that I already at the age of twelve drove backwards and forwards in the yard, out through the gate and about twenty meters further, in order to turn around in the neighbour's drive and then go back again.

All I had to do was ask permission, and then stick to the rules about not driving a meter farther than the agreement stipulated and everything was fine.

Among the various cars Max had after the war, there was, at this point, a used American Chrysler DeSoto with a sort of semi-automatic gear shift. This was a large solid vehicle and it was used, among other things, to pull a home-

155

made snowplough to clear the more than two hundred meter drive from the main road to the garage and then on to the main house. We had a lot of fun when this happened. The plough, which was toughed behind the car, had to be partly steered and kept down with weight, and we boys were always willing to do the job.

After serving my apprenticeship in the Morris, I was allowed in this, much bigger, American one. All this led eventually to my being an unregistered member of the Home Guard at fourteen or fifteen and being given the job of staff driver during exercises.

As one can understand, rules were handled a bit differently in those days, at least by Max; this, of course, to my great pleasure.

The practical part of my driving was thus accomplished several years before reaching the driving licence age limit. Max eventually also let me drive on public roads when he was sitting next to me, which quickly took care of the theoretical part as well.

In other words, when I at seventeen went to Italy and the Olivetti school there, I was, at least according to myself, ready as far as driving a car was concerned.

A Vespa-scooter was bought at the very beginning of my first year at Ivrea in Northern Italy.

I went from a technical education in the north to a commercial school in Florence.

The time of my eighteenth birthday is rapidly approaching. I had long ago located the relevant office in which to apply for a driving licence and was ready for action. What follows has to be seen in light of it being 1957, a light year away from a world full of modern communication and data.

I make my appearance on the fourteenth of May, my 18th birthday; in the driving licence office in plenty of time before it opens and sit down to wait.

I can't remember if queue numbers had been invented in those days, but regardless, the first person at the counter was yours truly. I show them my British passport and tell them that I come from Norway, explaining that I would like a driving licence.

The employee is friendly enough and asks to see my Norwegian driving licence. I had, of course, worked out my strategy and tell him without hesitating that in Norway a driving licence isn't necessary, that I'm attending the Olivetti school in Florence, am intending to buy a car and am thus in need of a driving licence to show, if asked. If he's heard of a country called Norway at all, I don't know, but even so, he probably has no idea on which continent it's situated.

I quickly tell him that I have driven since I was sixteen, rather than tell the truth, so as not to make it too hard to believe.

He is obviously unsure and turns to a colleague. Personally I believe that my attending the Olivetti School clinched the deal. In those days everything to do with Olivetti was in Italy filled with prestige. After having asked me if I intended to drive abroad, to which I answered 'yes' and explained that I wanted to drive back to Norway on holiday, he said it would then have to be an international driving licence.

He made it clear that the first thing to be done was to have a medical check-up.

This I could have done across the street. He pointed to an office on the other side of the wide avenue, which consisted of ten to fifteen meter pavements on either side with four lanes of traffic in the middle and with trees which looked like the chestnut trees in Bygdøy Allè in Oslo. With a statement from them, I could qualify. He handed me a note with the name of the doctor.

There was fortunately no queue, so everything looked fine. The doctor must have made several tests but the only thing I remember, and which was thoroughly done was having to read numbers on a board and then stretch out first the right leg and then the left, while rotating each foot in both directions.

Everything was all right, the form filled in, but still on his side of the counter he remained static holding a rubber stamp in his right hand. In the process of lifting the rubber stamp, his arm came to a stop and he looked at me. I looked back at him and his arm slowly lowered. The same thing happened once more, before I got the hint.

A few more banknotes were put on the counter; the rubber stamp was lifted into the air and landed on the right place on the paper. Smiles and handshakes followed by 'good luck'.

Back at the starting point there is now a small queue. We were approaching siesta time and several people leave, thinking they won't make it before closing time. I take no chance and keep waiting.

After a short time, I'm beckoned ahead and hand over the medical certificate. The same employee nods in recognition and says that now only the practical part remains. Since I'd already driven for two years, the theory was in his opinion not necessary, as the signs were more or less international. I simply had to demonstrate my driving skills.

With a form in my hand, I was sent to some premises down on the pavement, which on this side of the avenue and for a distance of about fifty meters only had a narrow passage for pedestrians, while the rest was blocked off for cars. I believe I was asked a few questions before I was placed in a small Fiat and asked to drive up to the barrier and reverse back. I didn't get further than second gear before I had to stop and go back.

Here there was also a question of having to pay something, but by now I'd learnt the trick. The rubber stamp was raised only once before it hit the paper and I could happily walk away with a "passed" stamped on my document.

Now it was just a question of formalities. The details regarding these had been postponed, as I might possibly have failed the practical test thus rendering them unnecessary. One has to be rational after all.

All the vital details were taken down till the last comma and when everything was done, I was told to come back the following day with the specified number of lire.

The next day dawns and with great expectations I appear once more in front of the counter. Has everything turned out all right or . . . ?

From a shoebox on the side table the employee pulls out an envelope which he opens with a smile, no problem – everything's fine. This time the amount in question was considerable, at least for me, I believe it was something like a hundred Norwegian kroner, so I had counted it out before handing it over. Now there was no rubber stamp involved but it was clear that the envelope wouldn't be handed over just like that.

As he fumbled around extra-long with the receipt, I went into action, whereupon he with an extra smile and a 'good luck' handed me the envelope which to me was gold worth. There I was with an international driving licence in my hand.

Before leaving Ivrea, I sold my Vespa for what was the equivalent of nine hundred kroner in those days and made a down payment of a couple of hundred on a Lancia Aprilia, the total price of which was eight hundred kroner. Including the cost of the driving licence of about one hundred kroner, that meant that the Vespa had been exchanged for a fully drivable 1949 model, which in Italy went by the name of "La Regina della Strada", which translates into English as "The Queen of the Road". It was in those days a very advanced car with a four cylinder V engine and plenty of horse power, but since this story has to do with my driving licence, we will have to put further episodes with and about all that in abeyance, until inspiration strikes and the memories surface.

Confidence

To make a rocky fell in a short spell is nonsense -
to build a bridge from east to west, gives the soul a rest.
The span being stretched is not of steel
but it ties together, just wait and feel.
GM

The Grandchild

May 2013

To Oscar George Manus-Aasmundtveit on the day of his Christening

To the one we're waiting for

The miracle will happen in April sometime,
your mother and father wear smiles sublime.
We all arrive in the same old way,
but mystery also works - we all can say.

This is for you who are about to appear,
they have counted to five, or so I hear.
Five on each hand and foot they say,
keep to your time and don't delay.

Your weight is correct - at two-thirds of the race,
you keep on kicking and controlling the pace.
We already know that you're a boy,
it can clearly be seen, the size of a toy.

May you be happy where you currently remain
without causing your mother too much pain.
Start your entrance when you're ready with a yell,
making your granddad feel happy and well.

This was written in February hence
your parents still wait in suspense.
Will you arrive on time – will all be well -
or will you be difficult, causing them hell?

To the one who has arrived

It all went well – you went along with our ploy
and behaved like the wished for dream of a boy.
You came a week late – a Taurus making us glad -
and by God you are a wonderful lad.

On the first of May you came into the light
and greeted the world with a gasp full of might.
You look like your granddad everyone says
so you'll be a great charmer one of these days.

You'll barely see summer take over from spring,
before heading South to encourage grandma to sing.
There you'll get vitamins in the sunlight
and sleep like an angel all through the night.

Two months will pass before you come back here North
to be greeted with hugs as kisses break forth.
Then you'll be ready to meet the fall
and from what I can see, you'll be on the ball.

Today you were given your name, my dear
which you always with honour will proudly air.
Aasmundtveit Oscar George Manus,
perhaps you'll become a real "Janus".

Take one look ahead and another look back
if you learn to do that, you'll be right on track.

Dear Oscar – we salute you and wish you luck on your way.

Here's to Oscar!

22.09.96
Janus. *In Roman Mythology, the God of gates, doors, passages, all beginnings and endings.*

The Hair

January 2013

The hair I'm thinking of is the kind we normally have on our heads. I say normally because at least among a number of us men, the mane has a tendency to shrink until it covers fewer parts of our heads or disappears altogether.

This seems to be a natural process for those it affects and isn't normally related to a lack of vitamins or any other form of illness.

I once again say normally, because we know that hair loss can be caused by such things as well.

There are several reasons why I restrict myself to the hair we normally have on our heads. It would be tempting to extend the subject, but then it might easily lead to discrimination. It would be simple to include other hair-covered areas, but even then it would be natural to exclude certain parts.

Yes, the hairy parts must for this reason be restricted. However, as long as I stick to the head, it can't be discrimination to mention facial hair, can it?

No other hairy body-parts can for this reason feel discriminated against, can they?

Men outwardly don't seem to be too concerned about the hair on their heads but deep down I wonder if that's true.

The first tube of Brylcreem in one's youth caused heated discussions in many homes, as did the Elvis hair style and, not to mention, the brothel creepers, called "tractor shoes" in Norway, which led to many a family fight.

I personally remember very well both the Brylcreem tube and the Elvis hair style, but the "tractor shoes" debate never took place in my home, as my parents' tolerance in this case turned to veto.

That was back then; many, many years ago.

I've often thought about why we men choose our hair style, I've worn a parting for as long as I can remember and even though my hair has thinned out considerably over the years and has become completely grey and covers less, I still wear it, the parting that is, on the left side.

That doesn't mean I'm left-wing or ever was, far from it, but it's always just been that way from the very beginning. Especially among the younger ones, it's mostly fashions and idols which determine their hair style.

How many "Ronaldos" aren't to be seen among us today in 2017 and how many tens of tons of styling gel aren't sold in order to achieve the comparison?

It's clear that Beckham too, as a role model, has made his mark on his disciples. Fine with me, however he chose tattoos to be his special style. It is probably not difficult to understand that I can't really identify with this habit.

I accept, of course, everyone's right to "dress up" the way they want to, and it is a known fact that our ancestors, partly for reasons of ritual, did the most incredible things to attract attention. That's not to say that those who equip themselves with tattoos turn back the clock. Tattoos have always existed and as with everything else, their popularity comes and goes.

At the moment they seem to me to be at the height of their popularity.

We don't know for sure if he, Beckham that is, had anything special in mind when he started "adorning" himself. Perhaps he had to satisfy Victoria's wishes or, I guess no one will ever know, was it an advanced sort of "stunt" to gain extra attention?

I'm about to get side-tracked. I'll have to stick to the hair, not that I don't like Beckham's hair style, on the contrary. Doesn't he normally wear a parting too, and isn't it also on the left side?

Women on the other hand, contrary to men, have a totally different relationship with their hair. Style and colour aren't two different ingredients, for them the two go together. What's to be chosen? A myriad of shades are available and as regards hairstyles, the range is never-ending.

Most of them seem to sort things out quite well in my opinion.

Personally I'm not especially thrilled when some women chose boys hairstyles, but that's none of my business, they must have their reasons for doing so.

By mentioning that I'm not thrilled when some women chose boys hairstyles, it`s not quite true. Only a few special women can actually look very attractive wearing them.

If one has lived in the South of Spain for some time, one has become spoiled when it comes to raven black, long hair; undoubtedly somewhat special.

As regards women and hair, we're talking big money.

Billions roll from the hopeful straight into the pockets of those who create the psychosis. It's not hard to see who can afford TV advertising, but as we know, business is business.

There's something about healthy hair reflecting a healthy body. Here there might be some discrepancies though, especially if the mane is a result of one of these miracle products. No, "one can't judge a book by looking at its cover".

Men's hairy faces seem to be a matter of fashion.

Women are always doing their utmost to get rid of the smallest hint of same, which is quite natural, whereas there is probably an army of men out there, speculating on how they would look with some sort of beard or moustache, or both for that matter.

Is there something one needs to offset by growing hair on one's face?

A becoming moustache can come in handy if one has an undershot bite, in the same way that both a beard and a moustache can show that one still has visible hair-growth even though one has run out of hair on one's head.

I personally am concerned that the hair at the back of my neck, which has a tendency to curl, shouldn't be cut too short. I have for as long as I can remember wanted it to have some volume there. Especially in the last ten to twenty years, I have always given clear instructions about it to my hairdresser. Can that have something to do with the fact that my bald spot is gradually, though not too quickly, increasing in diameter?

There has to be a lot of money to be made in hair products for men as well, which seems to prove that men are also getting increasingly concerned with their appearances. Lately I've noticed more and more adverts for products which are said to help men conserve their natural hair colour by keeping greyness at bay. It supposedly has nothing to do with dying one's hair but is just meant to keep the budding greys under control. I've never tried this variety as I've always been quite happy with the grey one.

In order not to keep anything back, I admit to using a shampoo which supposedly causes what remain of one's hair to stay grey and stops it from slipping into the white genre.

As can be seen from all this, I can't be considered exempt from having a touch of vanity as regards my hair.

The Hand

September 2012

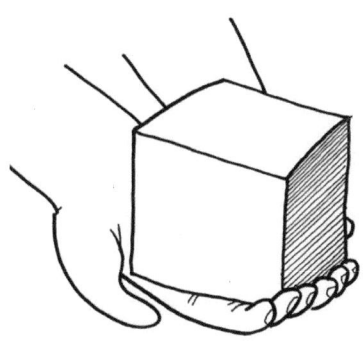

"Leave it in my hands", is a phrase inspiring confidence, strength and safety.

"Can I leave it in your hands?" This would show no self-confidence, strength or safety, just a question filled with the hope that someone else will agree to take the challenge and do the job.

This is, of course, not the same if it is a planned delegation made by a responsible leader. He or she only looks for a confirmation that the one selected feels at ease with the task and the responsibility.

Who was the first to use these expressions, or the Norwegian one that I appreciate so much: "Nothing enters a closed hand"? The symbolism is wide-ranging, it's quite clear that if one wants to get anywhere one basically has to be open.

"To have been dealt a good hand" doesn't necessarily mean that one is playing cards. Regardless of the context, the expression gives the impression of strength.

"Hand on the Bible" symbolizes seriousness, one is under oath.

With "your hand on your hearth", you show faithfulness, loyalty and love.

For those who believe in it, the laying on of hands is a true power and is performed as the expression says, with one's hands.

These expressions to do with hands must originally have been caused by the incredible versatility and strength of the hand.

The hand must, of course, be directed or it would be worthless. On its own it's powerless.

A pat on the back symbolizes approval, a pat on the backside something quite different.

What about a pat on the cheek? Doesn't it symbolize friendliness and love?

The hand is not only the end of the arm with its customary five fingers.

It is what one uses to greet someone with when one meets and what one waves with while saying good-bye. It's what one salutes with and what one scratches with.

Fingerprints are apparently still the surest way in which to identify someone apart from DNA, but they're not easily seen with the naked eye.

What would one do without the hand's index finger in those countries which have not progressed further in elections than to dip the finger in waterproof ink as proof that one has voted and only once, quite clever in fact.

One might wonder why it's always the index finger which is being used for this purpose, or is my observation in this respect, wrong?

None of the fingers seem to be unsuitable for the storage of all manner of rings, but ultimately it's the so-called ring finger which is the most popular for this purpose.

What about those who possess powers to read one's future, what would they do if they didn't have one's hand as a source of information. In what other parts of the body could they find one's lifeline?

It would be hopeless to list all the obvious uses of the hand, it would fill several encyclopaedias and never cover them all.

No, one has to make note of the special properties of the hands. For instance the surgeon's handling of his instruments, a pilot's control in the cockpit and the versatility of all the different types of craftsmen.

One could keep going forever, but I let The Hand end with a solid symbol of agreement, which can work both ways.

Either "I give you my hand on that" or "Give me your hand on that".

It isn't really important if one's experiences are good or bad as long as one learns from them.
GM

The Mouth

June 2012

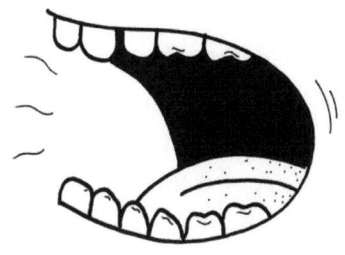

"My lips are sealed" is often used in situations where one possesses information which one would rather keep to oneself.

Unlike one's eyes, it's easy to keep one's mouth closed.

Apart from when one is asleep or meditating, it isn't easy to keep one's eyes closed for a long time.

One sort of feels excluded. It's far easier to observe, file away and dwell on impressions gleaned from one's surroundings with one's mouth shut. One can't close one's ears either, even though one at times would like to be able to.

Furthermore, there are normally two eyes and two ears and it would probably be too difficult if both, or for that matter all four had to be closed at the same time.

One doesn't normally focus one's attention on a closed mouth either, apart from the excitement one seems to remember feeling, or perhaps still feels, one's age taken into consideration, when contemplating a kiss. That excitement could be felt even when one's partner's mouth was initially closed.

If one excludes one's own unwillingness to speak or to disclose information one possesses, it is probably only through torture that one can be "persuaded" to talk.

No, normally it's the incredible interaction between mouth and voice one is fascinated by. I'm not thinking of the message the brain has planned or spontaneously wishes to express, but of the magic the interaction between voice and mouth really represents.

The result wouldn't be able to materialize without the mouth. Just think how incredibly flexible it must be.

The yawn is probably not the most beautiful of presentations, but a natural laugh can be both inspiring and contagious and, not least, a good laugh presents the mouth at its best.

We'll leave out the smile at the moment, as it has been deservedly dealt with in its own reflection.

The voice has also been given its own reflection, but when I now give thought to the mouth and the connection between all these wonderful senses, I see how finely tuned it all is.

I thought I included a lot in my reflection about the voice, but see now in retrospect that I completely forgot the role of the nose when it comes to the voice. Just try, pinch your nose closed and say the following sentence out loud: "This has become a total mess". The nasal influence is a necessary part of the voice. So now we understand the importance of the nose in the middle of it all as well.

The reflection about the voice was written in August 1995, while this one about the mouth has been added 17 years later. Have I learnt more about these senses since that time, something of importance? I certainly think so, without going further into it. I can only mention, that as the years accumulate, I have become more reserved when it comes to expressing myself firmly, at least outside my immediate surroundings.

I have, of course, become much wiser since then.

That I was born small-lipped hasn't prevented me at times from being "a big mouth".

If you're told that you're no good at this or that, take it as a compliment.
We can't all be good at everything.
If one is good at what one is good at, then we're all good in our own way.

GM

The Neck

April 2013

It's quite natural for us to have a neck, as where else could one's head be placed if not on top of our neck?

I have sometimes hear someone described as having their head between their shoulders, though I can't personally remember when. But we have probably all seen those who in despair pull their shoulders up so that it looks as if their heads are between their shoulders and not on top of their necks.

This normally happens for very short periods of time, so I can't really say it's something abnormal.

That some people have what's called a bull neck hasn't got anything to do with not having a neck but with the fact that the neck is the same width as the head all the way to the shoulders - such as with powerful bulls. Those who have become acquainted with the sport of rugby understand what I mean, but those who practice the sport and possess the above characteristic, also have muscles bulging in all directions, so that everything seems to be in proportion.

According to some, there are those who have their heads beneath their arms, but that is probably just an expression. One's head is placed where it is, and that's all there is to it.

When the description "headless" is used it is also not to be taken literally. We have all been equipped with a head and it's physically placed where it should be.

Why the head is placed at the highest point of human beings, should also be clear to most of us. As that is where the view or, perhaps more correctly put, the overview is at its best and that's important in all situations.

Our eyes and all the other vital senses of the different media are placed in the head. In other words, everything makes sense.

That one can have a proud neck is something I've wondered about.

Is that when the head is tossed and the neck moved in that special way, mainly perfected by the female part of the population? If that's the case, it apparently indicates, in addition to pride, something like being haughty and showing contempt. Oh well, I choose to see it as a sign of being unsure of oneself as well.

One obviously doesn't have to have a special type of neck in order to get a neck injury like whiplash. According to the insurance companies it is incredible how easily this, not clearly visible, condition can occur. Don't misunderstand me, for those affected, the condition can be both a long-lasting and painful challenge.

The French revolution from 1789 to 1799 is remembered by most of us more because of its use of the guillotine than for its political upheavals.

This very efficient method of separating the head of the poor victims from the rest of their bodies, wouldn't have been invented if not for the neck. Without it, it would have been practically impossible to perform the task. The neck means that it's easy to place the victim in a position where a perfect hit can't be avoided. A short process with one hundred per cent accuracy, at least as long as the mechanism works satisfactorily.

Oh well, that's probably not the reason the neck is placed where it is.

We can look upwards and downwards and to both sides by moving our necks, which is extremely practical as most of us don't have our eyes on stalks thus being able to move them in order to get the same perspective. Our ears also benefit from this as they are seemingly firmly placed where they are. Most of us hear better when the sound comes from the front.

In the animal world there are many species which are doubly equipped, both with a movable neck and ears and eyes which can be turned in all directions.

These abilities come in handy in the natural world for animals, of course, as one can thus avoid surprises and avert danger in time.

To pull oneself up by the neck, is a Norwegian expression which shouldn't be taken too literally. It would undoubtedly look strange if one stood there with one's arm at the back of one's neck trying to pull and tear at it to force oneself to do something which one for various reasons has put off doing. It's also important at times to grab oneself by the scruff of the neck, in order to stop oneself from doing something there and then, even though it would seem to be a natural reaction to do so.

Neck pain in general is quite widespread and it is said that thirteen per cent of the population will experience it. It is more common for women than men, for reasons unknown. Oh well, there can't only be advantages.

We golfers I expect are quite high in the statistics when it comes to neck problems. I believe there are few golfers who haven't at one time or other heard that little click which means that too much force has been put into a shot not made according to the textbook. Doesn't the explanation sound simple and straightforward?

Anyway, this millisecond of a swing can lead to weeks away from one's favourite hobby and is one of the few negative aspects of a golfer's life.

Duo

A symbol of our everyday condition
must be the smile in its standard position.
When one's need is at is greatest, one lives in hope,
but still will fight for the last sliver of soap.
GM

The Nose

September 2012

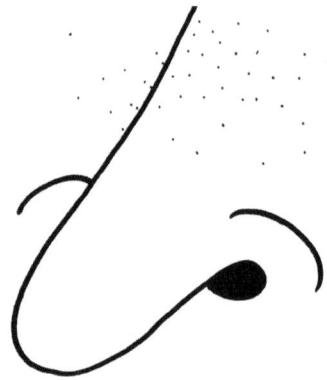

I don't understand why I've waited so long to write my reflection about the nose. It is after all one of our most characteristic features, where it normally sits, in the middle of our faces.

There's only one but with two channels- the nostrils. Why haven't we humans got two noses like our eyes or ears?

It is, of course, clear to me that there's nothing to indicate the need for a third dimensional effect when it comes to smell, which means we shouldn't need more than one.

Is it that simple? Probably not, but why does one have two channels, wouldn't one have sufficed?

It's probably just as well to have two, so that one is normally open to breathe through when the other for various reasons is stuffed up.

No, the nose is probably placed where it is so that one has something to put one's glasses on.

What would glasses have looked like if one had two noses, or if the nose had been placed in the middle of one's forehead?

It looks quite natural to me for the glasses to rest on the nose aided by the ears. Perhaps that's one of the reasons we have two ears. They do the job to perfection and one doesn't necessarily have to hear equally well in both ears for them to perform this job fairly well, quite brilliant, isn't it?

What would happen if glasses were made totally redundant and replaced by lenses or something similar, what would the nose be for but to smell with?

Perhaps it would then over millions of years degenerate and disappear.

Otherwise, it's usually in the way. Just think of the boxers, "The Noble Art of Self Defence". For them the nose is almost always in the way. Isn't there something about them removing the cartilage in the nose surgically so that it will yield to a direct hit? What about the Norwegian expression for having plenty of backbone which says: "to have bones in one's nose". Most people take this as a compliment but what about the boxers?

Another reason why it's sticking out is probably because if it didn't it would be more difficult to blow and one has to do a bit of a clean-up now and then.

Noses come in all categories, here I'll have to be careful.

The hooked one, characteristic for . . . ? The one referred to as aquiline. The snub nose, with its nostrils staring at you; wide ones, narrow ones, big and small, makes no difference to the sense of smell.

That there's a big difference in the sense of smell, however, is clear.

It's also clear that most animal species have a far better sense of smell than us humans, but then they also have differently shaped noses.

Once again, doesn't it seem perfectly logical? I have never seen animals wearing glasses, so why should they have noses like us? In this case it's the human being who has degenerated / deteriorated with a worse sense of smell and the need for glasses.

The most incredible nose of all is the one that has a tendency to grow in length when truth is tampered with. That nose only belonged to one fictional character, and he is unforgettable to us all, namely Pinocchio. His story was written by the Italian Carlo Collegio in 1883.

If that invention had been widespread among the human race, the struggle to invent the lie-detector would have been in vain.

Oh yes, the sense of smell improves the glass of wine or cognac brought to one's mouth, most noses are adapted to absorb the aroma along with the noble drops, when the glass is lifted to one's mouth. This is emphasized by the aromatic diversity of the cognac.

How would the glasses be shaped if they didn't have this property, or the nose look, if it wasn't able to handle this task?

If nature hadn't found a suitable solution to this problem, many of us would have looked differently on life.

As with the wine and cognac glass, there is in most cases an interaction between smiling eyes and an expression of satisfaction.

But only in most cases, as for instance a bad wine or for that matter other bad smelling drinks, will call forth other but clearly registrable expressions.

"Don't poke your nose into somebody else's business", probably isn't meant literally, but everyone understands its meaning.

"He or she has a nose for something". Also not meant to be taken literally, but states clearly that the person in question has a skill for whatever it might be.

I myself wear glasses these days, have bad hearing in my right ear and use a hearing aid. I'm thus quite happy with the arrangement as it is, especially with my nose, but also with my ears for supporting both my glasses and my hearing aid.

In my head

In my head there's a diode with thread -
and behind my look so quick, there's many a click.
To adjust, open and shut -
the free circulation must never be cut.
GM

Transitions and Milestones

April 2014

Transitions from something to something else happen throughout one's entire life. Milestones often refer to the separations between planning stages or the descriptions of projects. For me it's just as natural to use the expression milestone about special anniversaries in life, even if it's not quite in accordance with its definition, and celebratory speeches are often held at significant milestones to mark their importance.

The transition from being a nameless child to suddenly having a registered name happens on one's day of baptism. The transition from being in kindergarten to starting school is an anniversary and a milestone, not to mention when one later changes from one school to another. A number of other anniversaries throughout life turn into milestones, which are referred to later. One's confirmation is for many an important milestone, as is naturally enough the founding of a family, normally by getting married. Then it usually starts again with children, baptism and confirmation, before the cycle is repeated by the new generation.

Even though many couples live together without being married, most families are founded on registered marriages. A large percentage of these, however, are dissolved, but not so many that quite a few aren't still able to celebrate the milestones of both silver and golden anniversaries and, on rare occasions, even platinum ones; transitions and milestones once again.

The milestones in other types of relationships than marriages are, of course, just as important to those concerned, and there are probably no difference in the way the milestones are being celebrated.

Many see the transitions from one year to another as milestones and make the appropriate wishes for themselves and others.

The world is still large and not everyone celebrates that milestone on the same date. That is, of course, not important as long as it is highlighted.

Birthdays also belong here and are important milestones in order to keep track of development, but for most of us, they count less and less as we get more mature.

At first one wishes to grow up as quickly as possible, whereas later, at a mature age, one would have liked to have disc brakes with ABS to lower the speed.

It's this latest transition I would like to dwell on.

Since I'll be seventy-five in May this year and have become seriously acquainted with the repair age, I undeniably reflect upon development.

We all know that the so-called biological ascent normally reaches its high point around the age of forty. Then it gradually starts going downhill, whether one wants it to or not. Not that we become less efficient, or immediately notice that our bodies become less resilient or able to perform, the transition is normally so gradual that we're not aware of it and that's good; but that the transition takes place, there's no question about.

Why we don't normally become less efficient, is probably because we compensate with acquired experience and then, of course, there's the fact that we become wiser as we slowly but surely slip into a more mature age, or isn't that the case?

There are certain advantages to being "vintage".

I myself can't remember having had a so-called mid-life crisis. I was probably too busy to register it myself at least, but it's quite possible that others did.

For many this crisis can be quite serious and lead to big challenges both for those affected and their surroundings.

There are probably strongly diverging opinions on the highly personal mid-life crisis and what it actually represents. I am of the opinion that for many, and perhaps especially for women, the crisis, if it happens at all, comes as a result of the children now becoming independent. Having done everything for them as they were growing up, perhaps without having worked and created a collegial network to support her, she's left standing, slightly panicky, with a number of unsatisfied needs, which she would like to have met.

I don't believe anyone sees these examples as milestones to be celebrated, but it might be a good idea to do something to mark the day when one feels that they're over and done with, mightn't it?

Women's menopause doesn't come at a given time, but is said to appear somewhere between forty-five and fifty-five. It also doesn't disappear too quickly, so it is simply a situation both those affected and their surroundings must learn to live with.

That transition one normally bypasses without fuss and without making it into a milestone, doesn't one?

Within politics and government-related situations frequent references are made to transitions and milestones. Changes of government happen at regular intervals, normally from something existing to something new.

The transition turns into a real milestone when the change has to do with two political extremes. It is celebrated in grand style, at least on the winning side, even though most ordinary citizens don't even see it as a noticeable transition.

Important issues such as the vote for women and equality are examples of social matters which have to be taken seriously by the societies concerned and as the objectives are reached, they become milestones which are later referred to. Internationally, Norway is still seen as one of the world's most equality-minded societies.

When it comes to transitions to do with sport, the focus is mainly placed on football players who move from one club to another and the corresponding staggering amounts changing hands.

This doesn't mean that transitions don't happen in other sports than football, but we hear less about it.

In the meaning of anniversary and turning point, the transition from having two daughters to having only one was the biggest milestone in my life to date.

Life

I've lived life -
I've experienced life.
GM

Understanding

October 2013

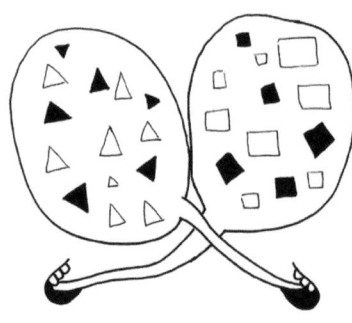

Think what a difference it would make if we humans one day really understood one another. This is, of course, not black and white, as we mostly understand one another at least as regards major issues, but differences and disputes often occur as a result of our thinking we have understood everything without this being the case; especially when it has to do with details, and small but important nuances.

There is usually no harm intended by either party, but often nuances cause misleading results.

Does this mean that we in general don't understand one another and that there would be a marked difference in results on the day when we really do manage to understand one another? Yes, I definitely believe so. We often don't understand one another and this leads to unforeseen challenges in our narrow everyday lives, as well as in a larger national, international and global context. First we must recognise what is meant by fully understanding one another.

Here it isn't just that we speak different languages. Misunderstandings can be fertile ground for disagreements, even when both parties communicating, seemingly speak the same language.

In simple communication the main issues are usually understood. Nuances and details, however, often count for more than one can imagine.

This is what we have to realize if any of the content in this reflection is to make sense. We have to realize that when one delves into a communication, nuances can easily be downplayed or disappear and the deeper meaning often is not evident or understood.

Many of us can't see this, which is probably only to the good, as we don't all have to delve so deeply into details.

I have my own experience when it comes to different languages and understanding.

My wife of the last fifteen years is Swiss and since she comes from Geneva her mother tongue is French.

I don't speak French and have for various reasons never had the inclination to learn this language, so our communication takes place in English, a language which for both of us, at the beginning of our lives, was not our own and in both cases had to be learnt.

She has lived in Spain for more than forty years and was married to an Englishman in more than twenty, whereas my English comes from school in Norway, living abroad in a predominantly English environment and also from business.

Her vocabulary is fairly extensive whereas mine is more limited. Despite this, our everyday communication, in my opinion, functions very well.

We have also been part of the "vintage" category for some time now, and this undoubtedly has its advantages as regards communication since maturity often means acquiring a larger degree of tolerance, at least according to one-self.

It becomes easier to make allowances for misunderstandings when one is communicating in a language which is foreign to both and when one has a smidgen of tolerance.

Understanding is not always positive, however.

The so-called know-it-all's, who supposedly understand everything, aren't necessarily entirely likeable, but this doesn't mean, of course, that those who have no understanding whatsoever, automatically can be labelled likeable.

Expressions like: I understand your point of view, or suchlike, are frequently used in diplomatic circles, where it often has to do with making approaches through give and take. When results are to be achieved through understanding and tact, details and nuances are important.

In political contexts, appeals are often made to show understanding, thus calling for diplomatic solutions.

Can we learn to understand one another better?

For me it's quite clear that we can, as long as we first acknowledge the fact that it is often understanding the details and nuances which make for a better relationship. If one is conscious of this one can in various contexts, through the seeking of common understanding, go a long way towards reaching more agreement.

Wrinkles

September 2012

What do wrinkles have to do with the Norwegian National Anthem? Directly, absolutely nothing, but certain associations come to mind.

The Norwegian National Anthem: "Ja, vi elsker dette landet", which in its literal translation reads: "Yes, we love this country", was written by Bjørnstjerne Bjørnson in 1859. Each verse begins with: "Yes, we love this country", and what I have in mind is the continuation of the first verse, which goes:

"Yes, we love this country as it rises forth, furrowed, weather-beaten above the water with its thousand homes".

The words furrowed and weather-beaten probably refer to the country itself and not so much to its people. I find it difficult to believe, however, that Bjørnson, at the time when he wrote the song, didn't have a clear idea that a country and its people in many ways merge into one.

Furrowed and weather-beaten, at the time when Bjørnson wrote the National Anthem and applied to the people, means to me staunchness, solidity and endurance.

Furrowed; I see the face of a person who during a long life has defied its many challenges and become weather-beaten as the result of having kept on going in all sorts of weather.

One is affected by it. Endurance is in many ways the same as never giving up and at the same time an important ingredient in the continuity of life.

In Norway one has to travel to remote parts these days to find people of the furrowed and weather-beaten variety, but they are there and I believe there are more of them than we think.

That's not to say that one has to be furrowed and weather-beaten to be staunch, solid and enduring. Life has just become more refined. Life's aspects are becoming greater in every way, in the same way that marketing over decades has produced more diverse fashions and trends.

I don't believe the fight against wrinkles among the average citizens was as widespread at the middle of the nineteenth century.

Even though it's generally accepted that a shirt ought to be free of creases /wrinkles, it doesn't mean everything has to be wrinkle-free in order to be good.

We all know that the ideal iron for smoothing one's face has yet to be invented and it is, after all, the wrinkles in their faces most women are concerned about, isn't it? Men, as far as I know, normally don't worry too much about it.

We have arrived at the heart of the matter. We all know that if one lives long enough, then the wrinkles will appear.

First off, perhaps the ones on one's forehead. Not always due to worries, they just appear naturally.

Then we've got the ones caused by smiling, those whose development one to a certain extent can influence. There must be a reason for calling them smile lines. Just go to the mirror and produce a smile. "Smile to the world and the world smiles back", it is said. Right enough, but the more you smile the more smile lines you get.

A bit later in the process, the wrinkles appear around one's mouth. They probably appear by themselves too, as a result of age, or as I prefer to call it, maturity.

What would one do if one, as if by magic, developed an iron which would make all the wrinkles disappear?

A smooth face above an old body. O.K., most of one's body one can hide with one's clothing, but always having to wear a high-neck sweater or a scarf can become tedious.

Just imagine the contrast between the creases / wrinkles which over time develop below one's chin and a completely smooth face.

Aha, someone will say. Wrinkles below one's chin and many of the ones in one's face, one can to a certain extent get rid of by so-called beauty interventions, or face-lifts, and that's true.

Every year, billions are being spent on creams and injections, vitamins and massages what nature has meant should accompany us until our last day; that is if we live long enough.

I am, of course, of the opinion that one should deal with these challenges as they appear, always bearing in mind that this is a natural process, which when wrongly interfered with can influence one's personality and seldom for the better.

An entirely different matter is that I believe a reasonable amount of wrinkles only accentuates one's personality.

****

Measuring

**We measure most things in what we get done
and what we don't get done.
In any case, we blame it on time when we are dissatisfied,
it's always time which is to blame - as if it's responsible for
our inability to organize ourself better.**

GM

Your own spirit determines your life.
GM

Nothing is better than a good conscience.
GM

Weapons alone seldom solve a crisis.
GM

It's only through one's own experience that one is able to progress.
GM